The Mystery of Monster Mountain

Alfred Hitchcock
and The Three Investigators in
The Mystery of Monster Mountain

Text by M. V. Carey

Based on characters created by Robert Arthur

Illustrated by Jack Hearne

Random House  New York

Library of Congress Cataloging in Publication Data:
Carey, M   V   Alfred Hitchcock and the three investigators in The mystery
of Monster Mountain.   (Alfred Hitchcock mystery series, 20)
SUMMARY: The three young sleuths solve a case of double identity while
investigating the legend of Monster Mountain.   [1. Mystery stories] I. Arthur,
Robert.   II. Hearne, Jack, illus. III. Title. IV. Title: The mystery of Mon-
ster Mountain. V. Series.
PZ7.C213Ald   [Fic]   73–3693
ISBN 0–394–82664–7   ISBN 0–394–92664–1 (lib. bdg.)

Contents

A Word From Alfred Hitchcock

Greetings, mystery lovers!

Once again I have the pleasure of introducing that team of youthful sleuths known as The Three Investigators. "We Investigate Anything" is their slogan, and so they do. Usually they conduct their operations out of their official Headquarters—an abandoned mobile home trailer in The Jones Salvage Yard in Rocky Beach, a small community not far from Hollywood. This time, however, they journey to the high slopes of the Sierra Nevada for an adventure which begins simply, with a search for a missing key. Complications are soon piled on complications as the lads learn the strange secret that threatens the woman called Anna, and discover the truth behind the dark legends of a hermit and a monster.

In the event that any of our readers are meeting The Three Investigators for the first time, I shall only say that Jupiter Jones, the First Investigator and leader of the group, is a stout fellow with an extremely agile mind and a remarkable talent for scenting trouble. Pete Crenshaw is the tallest and most athletic of the trio. Though he is never a coward, he does cherish a sensible desire to keep out of danger. Bob Andrews, quiet and studious, keeps records for the group, and has a flair for research which is invaluable to The Three Investigators.

Now that the introductions are completed, the reader will please turn to Chapter One. Monster Mountain awaits!

ALFRED HITCHCOCK

The Mystery of Monster Mountain

1

Sky Village

"Wow!" said Pete Crenshaw when he first saw Sky Village. "This place looks like a stage set. Somebody should make a movie here!"

Bob Andrews was kneeling beside him in the back of the pickup truck, looking over the roof of the cab at the village street. "Well, it won't be Mr. Hitchcock," he said. "This town is too darned wholesome for a mystery movie."

Jupiter Jones pulled himself to his knees beside Bob and planted his chubby arms on the top of the cab. "Mr. Hitchcock knows that mysteries can occur in all sorts of places," he reminded his friends. "But you're right. Sky Village is very new and artificial."

The truck ground up the steep grade of the street and passed a ski shop that resembled a cottage in the Alps. Next to the ski shop was a motel which had a roof of imitation thatch. Now, in midsummer, the ski shop and the motel were closed. Bright blue shutters covered the windows of a restaurant called The Yodelerhaus. A few pedestrians strolled along the sunny sidewalks and, in a gas station, an attendant in faded denims dozed in a chair.

The truck turned into the gas station and stopped near the pumps. Hans and Konrad got out of the cab. The two Bavarian brothers had worked for Jupiter's Aunt Mathilda and Uncle Titus for years. They helped sort, clean, repair, and sell items which Uncle Titus acquired for The Jones Salvage Yard. The brothers were always neat and tidy when they came to work. Today they surpassed themselves. Hans wore a new sport shirt which had not a wrinkle in it, even after the long drive from Rocky Beach through the Owens Valley and up to the ski resort high in the Sierra Nevada. Konrad's slacks still held their press, and his shoes gleamed.

"They want to make a good impression on their Cousin Anna," whispered Bob to Jupe.

Jupe smiled and nodded. The three boys watched from the back of the truck as the Bavarian brothers approached the sleeping gas station attendant.

"Excuse me," said Hans to the man.

The man grunted and opened his eyes.

"Please," said Hans, "where is the home of Anna Schmid?"

"The Slalom Inn?" The man stood up and pointed toward a grove of pines which edged the street. "Go past those trees and you'll see a white house on your left. You can't miss it. It's the last place before the road turns off to the campground."

Hans thanked him and began to get back into the truck.

"Is Anna expecting you?" asked the man. "I saw her drive down the road toward Bishop a couple of hours ago. I don't think she's back yet."

"Then we wait for her," said Konrad.

"Could be a long wait," said the man. "Nearly everything in Sky Village is closed for the summer, so Anna's probably got big shopping to do in Bishop."

"It has already been a long wait," said Konrad cheerfully. "We have not seen Anna since we were children together, back home, before we come to the United States."

"Well, well!" exclaimed the man. "Friends from home, eh? Anna will be real pleased."

"Not friends," said Konrad. "Family. We are Anna's family—her cousins. Now we come to surprise her."

"Hope she likes surprises," said the man. Then he chuckled. "Hope you do, too. Anna's been busy these last couple of weeks."

"Oh?" said Hans.

"You'll find out." The man's eyes sparkled. He reminded Jupiter of several of Aunt Mathilda's friends who collected tidbits of gossip about their neighbors in Rocky Beach.

Hans and Konrad got back into the truck.

"I have a feeling that guy doesn't miss much," said Pete as they drove off.

"He probably doesn't have much to do in the summer except keep an eye on everybody who goes up and down this road," decided Bob. "Once the snow's gone, how many customers can he have?"

The truck went slowly up the village street. They passed an ice-cream shop, which was open, and a drugstore, which was closed. The Sky Village General Market was dark, and so was a gift shop.

"I wonder what's kept Cousin Anna so busy," said Pete. "This place is really dead."

"From what Hans and Konrad have told me," said Jupe, "their cousin can always find something profitable to do. She came to the United States ten years ago and got a job as a maid in a New York hotel. Hans says that in six months she was in charge of the entire housekeeping staff, and in only six years she'd saved enough money to buy a little inn here in Sky Village. A year later she purchased a ski lift, and that must pay handsomely when the snow comes."

"She did all that on a housekeeper's salary?" said Pete.

"Not quite. She had a second job, part-time, and she invested in good stocks. She is a smart businesswoman, and Hans and Konrad are very proud of her. They read all of her letters out loud to anyone who will listen, and their rooms are full of snapshots she's sent them. When Aunt Mathilda and Uncle Titus suddenly decided to close the salvage yard for two weeks and take a holiday, they jumped at the chance to come up here."

"I'm glad they did," said Pete. "How else would we have got away for a camping trip? I've been wanting to try some rock climbing, and I hear the Sky Village Campground is great—and never crowded."

"Too far from the superhighways," said Bob.

"I just hope Cousin Anna doesn't mind surprises," said Jupe. "Hans and Konrad tried to call her before we left, but she wasn't home. Of course, they're prepared to camp out with us, so they won't be imposing on her."

The truck labored on and up, through the grove of pines which the gas station attendant had pointed out. Once they were beyond the pines, the boys could see a ski slope. It was a barren brown cut on the east side of the mountain, as bare as if some giant had shaved the hill clear of any tree or shrub that might interfere with the downward rush of the skiers. Running up the slope was a series of steel towers connected by cables. Every twenty feet or so, a chair dangled from the cables.

The truck pulled over to the left side of the road and stopped in front of a big white house that almost backed into the ski slope. A sign in front announced that this was the Slalom Inn.

"I see that Cousin Anna is still a good housekeeper," said Bob.

The inn was a trim wooden building, white-painted and glowing in the afternoon sun. The windows were so crystal-clean that they were almost invisible. Unlike many of the buildings in Sky Village, Anna Schmid's inn did not try to look Swiss or Austrian. It was simply a mountain lodge with a broad porch across the front. The door had been painted bright red, and plants in red and blue pots marched along the porch railing.

There was a neat gravel drive on the left side of the house, and a small parking area which contained a dusty station wagon and a shiny red sports car.

Hans and Konrad climbed out of the truck and the boys scrambled down from the back.

"I think Anna has done well," decided Hans.

"Anna always did well," said Konrad. "You remember when she was only ten she could bake better pastries than our mother. We always wanted to go to Anna's and have hot chocolate and pastries."

Hans smiled. The sun had started to dip toward the cliffs above the ski slope and the thin mountain air was cool. "Let's go in. We will wait for Anna to come back from her big shopping, and perhaps she will have some pastries for us."

Hans and Konrad started up the steps to the porch. Jupiter, Pete, and Bob stood where they were.

"You aren't coming?" asked Hans.

"Maybe we should get on to the campground," said Bob. "You haven't seen your cousin for a long time, and we don't want to intrude."

Hans and Konrad both laughed. "How can you intrude?" said Hans. "You are no strangers. We have written to Anna and told her the smart things you do. She says you are clever boys. She always writes that we must come and see her, and she wants us to bring you."

So the three boys followed Hans and Konrad up the steps. The front door was unlocked. It opened directly into a huge room which was furnished with deep leather chairs and a long, leather-covered sofa. There were shining copper lamps and, above a stone fireplace on the far wall, gleaming pewter mugs. Four places had been set at a big dining table on the right; behind it was the door to the kitchen. On the lefthand wall, a rustic staircase led up to the second floor. The room smelled of wood fires and furniture polish, and there was a faint trace of an odor that made Jupe think Anna still baked very good pastries.

"Anna?" called Hans. "Anna, are you home?"

No one answered.

"So we wait," said Konrad. He began to roam about the room, touching the backs of the leather chairs. He beamed with satisfaction. "Everything is very good," he said. "Yes, Anna has done well."

But then his wanderings brought him to a door in the wall to the right. Though it had a sign which read "Private, No Admittance," the door stood open. Konrad looked in and said, "Ho!"

"Ho, what?" Pete wanted to know.

"I think that nobody is perfect," said Konrad, "not even our Cousin Anna."

Hans went to stand beside his brother, and he shook his head in mock dismay. "Anna, Anna! We will tease you about this. Jupe, look at the office of the great housekeeper."

"Maybe you'd better not look at the office," advised Pete. "My mother has a fit if I open her desk or look in her pocketbook."

Jupiter Jones was about to settle down in one of the chairs when suddenly Hans turned to face him. "Jupe," he said. "Bob. Pete. I think something is wrong here!"

"What is it?" Jupe went to the door and looked into

a little room which was obviously the office of the inn. A large desk, covered with papers, faced the door. A file cabinet stood nearby with two drawers open. File folders and papers were dumped helter-skelter on the floor, together with the crumpled debris from an overturned wastebasket. The drawers were out of the desk and leaning against the wall. The window sill behind the desk chair was a jumble of envelopes, snapshots, and picture postcards. A bookcase had been pulled out from the wall, and an overturned dish spilled a stream of paper clips across the floor.

"This place has been searched!" said Pete, who was right behind Jupe.

"It would seem so," said Jupe, "and by someone who was either very careless or in a great hurry."

"Just what do you think you're doing?" snarled a husky voice from the big room behind them.

The boys spun around.

A man stood near the stairs—holding a shotgun!

2

Cousin Anna's Surprise

"Okay. Speak up. What are you doing?" The man near the stairs made an impatient movement and the gun in his hands swerved. Pete ducked instinctively.

The man advanced several steps. He was tall and broad-shouldered, with thick, dark hair. His eyes looked very hard and very cold. He trained the gun on the group huddled by the office door. "Speak up!" he demanded again menacingly.

"Who . . . who are you?" said Konrad. He couldn't take his eyes off the gun.

The man didn't answer. Instead, he repeated his question. "What are you doing? Can't you see that room is private? I ought to—"

"One moment!" Jupiter Jones' voice cut into the tirade. Jupe stood as tall as he possibly could. "Perhaps you would care to explain yourself," he said in the haughtiest tone he could manage.

"What?"

"It appears that this place has been searched," said Jupe. "The police might be interested in knowing what *you* are doing here and why you are so quick with a gun."

Jupiter was in no position to summon the police, and he knew it. However, his air of command bewildered the man with the gun. He frowned and lowered his weapon until it pointed toward the floor. "You want the police?" he said.

"It seems to me that the proper thing to do would be to summon them," said Jupe in his precise fashion. "On the other hand, it might be wiser to wait until Miss Schmid returns from Bishop and have her make the complaint."

"Miss Schmid?" said the man. Then he laughed. "Let me fill you in on a few things," he said.

Just then a car door slammed outside. There were quick footsteps on the porch. The front door opened and a tall woman came in carrying a sack of groceries.

"Cousin Anna!" said Hans.

The woman stood still. Her eyes went from the man with the gun to Hans and Konrad, then to the boys, then back to the man with the gun.

"Cousin Anna?" said Hans again. This time it sounded like a question.

"Cousin Anna?" said the man with the gun. "Good heavens! You must be Hans and Konrad from Rocky Beach! I didn't recognize you from the snapshots Anna

showed me. Why didn't you say something? I might have shot you."

"You are a friend of Anna?" asked Konrad.

"You might say so. Anna, you didn't write to your cousins. You promised me you'd write to them before we went to Lake Tahoe."

"Oh! Hans and Konrad!" The woman put the groceries down on a table, touched one hand to the thick blond braids which were wound around her head, then smiled a broad smile. "Hans and Konrad!" She held out both hands to Hans, who went to her and kissed her on the cheek.

"It has been so long," she said.

Konrad elbowed his brother aside and kissed her, too.

"And look at you!" said Anna. "Such big strangers! I cannot tell." She turned from one to the other. "No. Even though you send me pictures, I cannot tell which is Hans and which is Konrad." Her voice was warm and full of amusement. She spoke quickly, almost without accent.

The brothers laughed and introduced themselves. They then presented Jupiter, Pete, and Bob.

"You have written me about these clever ones," said Anna.

"Very smart boys," Hans assured her.

Konrad said something in German and patted Jupe.

Instantly, Anna's smile vanished. "We will speak English," she said.

Again Konrad spoke in German.

"I know," said Anna. "It is more like home if we

speak German, but we will speak English, if you please." She went to the man who still stood near the stairs and put her arm through his. "My husband does not speak German. We will not be rude to him."

"Your husband?" said Konrad.

"Anna!" exclaimed Hans. "When did you—"

"Last week," said the man. "Anna and I were married in Lake Tahoe last week. My name's Joe Havemeyer."

There was a moment of stunned silence. Then, "So that's Cousin Anna's surprise!" said Pete.

Anna laughed. Hans and Konrad hugged her and wished her well, and she showed them her wedding ring—a plain band of gold that fit loosely on the third finger of her left hand. Joe Havemeyer accepted the brothers' congratulations.

Jupiter Jones hated unfinished business and unsolved mysteries. He waited until the laughter and the exclamations had run their course, then stepped into the office of Anna's little inn and beckoned Anna to follow him.

"Look," he said, waving a hand at the jumble of papers scattered on the floor. "Someone must have come in while you were away and searched this room. You may want to call the police, or—"

Cousin Anna laughed. "Oh, that is funny. Hans and Konrad have written that you are a detective. That is very funny."

Jupe did not enjoy being laughed at. He felt his face getting hot, and he scowled.

"No, no. Do not be angry," said Anna. "I think you

are a good detective. You are right. This room has been searched. My husband and I, we searched it."

Jupiter waited, not speaking.

"You see," said Anna, "I have lost a key. It is an important key and I must find it, so I looked everywhere."

"Maybe we can help," offered Pete. "At least, maybe Jupe can help. He's very good at figuring out where people put things."

"And we're awfully good at searching," added Bob. "Jupe, do you have one of our cards that you can give Miss Schmi . . . I mean, Mrs. Havemeyer?"

Jupiter was still slightly annoyed that Anna had laughed at him, but he took out his wallet and fingered through it until he found a card, which he handed to Anna. It read:

THE THREE INVESTIGATORS
"We Investigate Anything"
?   ?   ?

First Investigator .... Jupiter Jones
Second Investigator .... Peter Crenshaw
Records and Research .... Bob Andrews

Anna looked at the card. "Very nice," she said.

"Thank you," said Jupiter stiffly. "We have an enviable record. We have succeeded in solving puzzles that have bewildered people far older than we. The question marks on the card symbolize the unknown, which we are always willing to pursue."

Joe Havemeyer grinned at Hans. "Does he always talk that way?" he asked.

"You mean like a book?" said Hans. "Jupe reads all kinds of things, and he can find out what happens, sometimes, when no one else can tell. You let Jupe look for your key and he will find it."

"That's very kind," said Joe Havemeyer, "but I don't think we need a firm of junior-grade detectives to find a missing key. It's here, so it's bound to turn up."

Without a word, Anna handed the card back to Jupe.

"Very well," said Jupe. "The key probably *will* turn up. In the meantime, we had better be moving. It gets dark early on this side of the Sierras and we want to get to the campground and pitch our tent while we can still see what we're doing."

"We go, too," said Hans. "In a little while we can come back and visit some more, huh?"

"Oh, no!" said Joe Havemeyer heartily. "Anna, we didn't have a wedding celebration. Now that your cousins are here, why don't we have a party? And Hans and Konrad don't have to camp out. We've got an empty room. They can stay with us."

Anna appeared startled at the idea, and Hans, who was watching her face, began to object. Konrad quickly interrupted his brother. "It will be a good idea for us to be here," he said firmly. "Anna's father is dead."

"Yes, Anna told me," said Joe Havemeyer. "What about it?"

"So she has no father to watch out for her," Konrad went on. "We are her only family here, and some relative should speak for Anna."

He turned to his cousin and said something in German.

"We speak English, please," Anna snapped. "Also, if you want to speak with Joe about me, you should have done it before we got married. That is the proper time."

"But Anna, you did not tell us you would be married," said Konrad reasonably.

"There is no need to tell you. There is no need to worry. Joe has a good income. And he will stay here in Sky Village and help me run my inn. In the winter he will manage the ski lift. It is all decided and it is not your place to make speeches."

Konrad turned red and lapsed into silence. Joe Havemeyer made soothing sounds to Anna. She went off to the kitchen with her groceries, and she did not look at either of her cousins as she left the room.

"I think we should leave," said Hans sadly.

"Come on, now," said Havemeyer. "Don't take it seriously. Anna's got a quick temper, but by dinnertime she'll be her usual cheerful self again. I know she's glad to see you. She's told me a lot about you. It's only that she's proud of being independent. She didn't like it when you acted like a heavy male relative."

Konrad rubbed his hand across his face. "I am stupid," he said. "It is that I have not seen Anna since she was so young, and suddenly I think I am her father, huh?"

"That's it exactly," said Havemeyer. "It'll be all right. You'll see."

Havemeyer was right. By dinnertime, Hans and Konrad had moved their luggage into the big square room on the north side of the inn. Since there were only four bedrooms in the place, and since two were already occupied by paying guests, The Three Investigators pitched their tent under the pines on the right side of the house, to the north. Joe Havemeyer had insisted on this. The stream that ran through the campground was low, he told them, because there had been very little snow and rain during the year. The boys would be better off if they stayed close to Anna's little inn—and a reliable source of water. Havemeyer also insisted that the boys join them for dinner that night. The two paying guests would have to be included in the family party, said Havemeyer, but he wouldn't let Mr. Jensen and Mr. Smathers spoil things.

The boys met Mr. Jensen and Mr. Smathers just before dinner. Mr. Smathers was a skinny little man who might have been fifty and who might have been older. He wore shorts and had hiking boots that laced almost to his knobby knees. Mr. Jensen was younger and taller and heavier, with close-cropped brown hair and a face that was homely but not unpleasant.

When Anna carried the roast in from the kitchen, Mr. Smathers made disapproving sounds with his tongue, then said, "Beef!"

"No lectures, please," said Mr. Jensen. "I'm very fond of roast beef and I'd appreciate it if you didn't make me feel like a murderer every time I pick up a fork."

"Animals are our friends," said Mr. Smathers. His watery blue eyes were fixed on Mr. Jensen. "Friends do not eat one another."

Anna had plainly regained her good humor. She smiled at Smathers. "I did not know the cow who was kind enough to provide our dinner. Let us not worry for him, since now he is at least not unhappy."

"Cows are female," Smathers pointed out.

"That is of importance only to the cow. For you I have creamed spinach and raw carrots and alfalfa sprouts."

"Excellent." Mr. Smathers tucked his napkin into his shirt front and prepared to enjoy his vegetarian dinner, while Mr. Jensen watched Joe Havemeyer carve the roast.

"Ever think of serving venison in season?" Jensen wanted to know. "I got a couple of good shots of deer on the road to Bishop this afternoon."

"Shots?" echoed Bob.

"Mr. Jensen is a carnivorous animal," said Smathers. "He would gladly shoot deer with a gun if it weren't against the law. Fortunately it is against the law, so Mr. Jensen does his shooting with a camera."

"I'm a professional photographer," explained Jensen. "I specialize in animal pictures. There are plenty of magazines that pay good money for authentic wildlife shots."

"Living off other creatures, just like any predator," said Mr. Smathers.

"I don't hurt them," protested Jensen. "I only take their pictures."

Smathers sniffed.

Joe Havemeyer finished carving and handed a platter of sliced meat down the table. "Mr. Smathers came up to hike in the high country," he explained to Hans and Konrad and the boys. "He's given me a real inspiration. Up above the ski run there's a meadow, and above that there are miles of real wilderness country. We're going to try to get hikers to come here in the summer. We'll advertise good food and good beds within a mile of nature's unspoiled domain."

Mr. Smathers looked up from his alfalfa sprouts. "It won't stay unspoiled for long if you do that."

"A few hikers won't disturb the birds and the bears that much," said Havemeyer. "In fact, the bears aren't a bit shy."

"Just because one got into the trash last night . . ." began Mr. Smathers.

"Spilled it all over the backyard," said Havemeyer.

"It isn't their fault," countered Smathers. "It's been too dry this year. There isn't enough forage for them in the high country, so they come into the village. Who's got a better right? The bears were on this mountain before the villagers were."

"Not this particular bear," said Havemeyer. "And he'd better not come back."

"Barbarian!" exclaimed Smathers.

Cousin Anna struck the table with her fist. "Enough!" she cried. "Tonight we have a party for my wedding and it will not be spoiled by a quarrel."

An uncomfortable silence settled over the group. Jupe, casting about in his mind for some neutral subject of conversation, thought of the excavation he had noticed that afternoon behind the inn.

"Are you planning to build an addition to the inn?" he asked Anna. "Someone's been digging out in back. Is it for a foundation for another building?"

"It will be a swimming pool," said Havemeyer.

"Swimming pool?" Hans was startled. "You want a swimming pool here? It is cool for swimming."

"It can get hot in the middle of the day," said Havemeyer. "Of course, it'll be a heated pool. When we advertise for the hikers, we can throw in not only nature's unspoiled domain, but also a refreshing dip in the pool at the end of the day. We might even roof the pool over and use it during the winter. Imagine skiing and swimming on the same day!"

"You think big, don't you?" said Mr. Jensen. There was a bite to his words that caught Jupe's attention.

"Something bothering you?" asked Havemeyer.

Before Jensen could answer, there was a metallic clattering from the back of the inn, then the crash of a garbage can being overturned.

Havemeyer pushed back his chair and strode to the little closet under the stairs.

"Don't!" shouted Smathers.

Havemeyer turned away from the closet. He had a sophisticated-looking gun in his hands.

"No, you won't!" Mr. Smathers jumped up and raced for the kitchen.

"Stop that, Smathers!" Havemeyer hurried after the little man. Hans, Konrad, and the boys followed. They were in time to see Smathers snatch open the back door.

"Go away!" cried Smathers. "Hide! Keep away!"

Havemeyer seized Smathers by the arm and yanked the little man out of the way. The boys had a fleeting glimpse of a large, dark shape fleeing toward the trees that edged the ski slope. Then Havemeyer was in the doorway. He threw up his gun and aimed. The gun made a little pinging noise.

"Blast!" said Havemeyer.

"Missed him, didn't you?" exulted Mr. Smathers.

Havemeyer stepped back into the kitchen. "I ought to belt you!" he told Smathers.

Pete touched Jupe's arm and headed for the living room.

"Did you see that gun?" whispered Pete before they returned to the dinner table.

Jupiter nodded. "A tranquilizer gun," he said softly. "Odd. Why go after a bear with a tranquilizer gun when there's a shotgun in the house?"

3

The Night Prowler

Jupiter Jones wiggled his toes against the lining of his sleeping bag and stared into the darkness. "The Three Investigators have a case!" he said aloud.

Bob lay next to Jupe in the tent. He turned over and hoisted himself on one elbow. "Do we get to hunt for Cousin Anna's key after all?" he asked.

"No. Hans and Konrad talked to me after dinner. They want us to investigate Cousin Anna's new husband. They are very uneasy about him."

Next to Bob, Pete yawned loudly. "I'm a little uneasy about him myself," he said. "The guy's gun-happy. I mean, all we were doing this afternoon was looking at the office and he practically threatened to shoot us."

"And he used a tranquilizer gun to scare off a bear," said Jupiter. "That makes no sense at all. Why would

24

he even own a tranquilizer gun? But it isn't the guns that are worrying Hans and Konrad, it's the swimming pool. They are afraid that their hard-working, practical cousin has married a man who'll fritter away her money on silly projects. I think we must agree that a swimming pool will not be an asset to an inn with only three guest rooms. It couldn't pay for itself.

"Hans and Konrad are also disturbed by the fact that Havemeyer has no job. They feel that a man his age should be working. While he was helping them move their things into the inn, he told them that he had inherited money from his family, and that he lived in Reno until he met Anna and decided to marry her. The red sports car in the parking lot is his, and it has Nevada plates, so that part of his story checks out."

"What do we do?" asked Pete. "Go on to Reno and talk to his former neighbors?"

"I hardly think that will be necessary," said Jupe. "Bob, does your father know anyone in Reno?"

Bob's father was a newspaperman in Los Angeles, and he knew other newsmen in many of the cities in the West. "Reno?" said Bob. "No, I don't think I've ever heard him mention anyone in Reno. But I could ask Dad to have the credit bureau in Reno report on Havemeyer. If Havemeyer ever opened any kind of a charge account, the credit bureau will have a file on him. Dad says credit files give you loads of information about people—where their bank accounts are and how much money they have and whether they pay their bills on time—lots of stuff."

"Good," said Jupiter. "We can call your father tomorrow." He sat up and lifted the tent flap. Across the yard, all the windows of the Slalom Inn were dark except one. "Joe Havemeyer is in Anna's office," reported Jupe.

"I guess he doesn't have to pay attention to that No Admittance sign," said Pete. He sat up, too, and peered out of the tent.

Through the uncurtained window of the office, the boys could see Cousin Anna's husband. He sat at the desk with his back to the window, sorting papers and putting them into file folders.

"Tidying up," said Pete. "I'm surprised Cousin Anna isn't doing that. She's supposed to be so neat."

"I think I am a little disappointed with Cousin Anna," said Jupe. "I'm afraid Hans and Konrad are, too. She didn't seem pleased when Havemeyer asked them to stay at the inn. She won't speak German with them. In fact, she doesn't talk to them much. She lets her husband do all the talking."

"Family reunions don't always turn out as advertised," Pete remarked. He had gotten into his sleeping bag wearing jeans and a warm sweatshirt. Now he fumbled in the dark for his shoes. "At least Cousin Anna's pastries lived up to their reputation," he said. "Since Havemeyer's up, I'm for going over to the inn. I could use a glass of milk and something to nibble on."

"You would mention food," Jupe moaned, but he too began to put on his shoes.

Bob unzipped his sleeping bag. "Count me in."

"Wait!" said Jupe suddenly. "Listen!"

Bob and Pete froze. There was a soft sound behind the tent, half growl and half inquiring whimper.

"A bear!" whispered Pete.

"Don't move," cautioned Jupe.

A twig snapped and there was a little scrabbling noise as if a fallen pine cone had been kicked aside. The animal came into sight and paused in front of the tent. The boys could see it silhouetted against the light from the office window. It was indeed a bear, a large, hungry bear. It sniffed in their direction.

"Go away!" whispered Pete frantically.

"Shhh!" warned Bob. "Don't frighten him!"

The bear was motionless, staring at the three boys. They held themselves as still as statues and stared back. Presently the bear seemed to lose interest in the tent and its occupants. It sneezed and ambled off toward the back of the inn.

"Whew!" Pete let out a sigh of relief.

"He only wants to raid the trash," whispered Bob.

Seconds later they heard a crash as a garbage can was overturned. Through the window of the office they saw Joe Havemeyer leap up and start for the door. Before he had gone three steps, however, there was a flash of blue-white light from the back of the inn. A second later the boys heard a wild yelping, and then a cry—a human cry!

The Three Investigators scrambled out of their tent and raced for the back of the inn. They skidded around the corner of the building in time to see the bear, a dark shadow, lumbering up the ski slope. From the

trees to the south of the inn came the sound of branches breaking, as if someone or something were running blindly through the thickets.

The light over the back door snapped on and the door crashed open. Joe Havemeyer burst out onto the small back porch, his tranquilizer gun ready. He glared down at the boys, then at the contents of the over-turned trash can which were sprayed wildly around at the bottom of the steps. Then he gasped.

Mr. Jensen, the nature photographer, was sprawled face down amid the litter. He was wearing pajamas and a bathrobe, and one slipper had come off. His camera lay beside him, smashed to bits.

"What the . . . ?" cried Havemeyer.

"You had a prowler," said Jupe. He bent over the fallen photographer. "A bear. I'm afraid Mr. Jensen is hurt!"

4

One Bear or Two?

Joe Havemeyer put down his gun and knelt beside the unconscious Jensen. "Did you see what happened?" he asked the boys.

"We saw a bear go past our tent," said Bob. "He went around to the back of the house, and we heard the trash can go over. Then we saw a flash of light and we heard the bear yelp, and then Mr. Jensen yelled."

Inside the inn, lights went on in every room. Cousin Anna appeared in the doorway. "Joe? What is it?"

"Jensen," said Joe shortly. "Tried to take a flash photo of a bear and got belted. We'd better get him to a doctor."

Mr. Smathers pushed through the door behind Anna. His sparse gray hair stood on end, and he had his bathrobe on inside out. "What seems to be the trouble?" he demanded.

Hans and Konrad followed Mr. Smathers out and came down the porch steps. "So?" said Hans. "What is happening?"

Jensen moaned, rolled over, curled his knees to his chest, and finally managed to sit up.

Havemeyer sat down on the steps, looking very frightened and, at the same time, very relieved. "You okay?" he asked Jensen.

The photographer made a grimace and put his right hand to his neck. "Someone . . . someone hit me," he said.

"I think you're lucky you're still breathing in and out," said Havemeyer. "Some people who get whopped by bears don't survive the experience."

Jensen got to his knees, then stood up and leaned against the wall of the inn. "I got whopped all right," he said. He shook his head as if to clear it. "I got whopped, but not by that bear. Somebody sneaked up behind me and belted me in the neck."

"Oh, come on now," said Havemeyer. "It had to be the bear. You scared it with your flash bulb and it took a swipe at you. They can move fast, you know."

"I know they can, but this one didn't. I saw it from the window in my room, so I got my camera and came down. I was aiming at the bear when I heard someone behind me. Then the flash went off, and a second later —whammo!"

Jensen straightened and glared at Mr. Smathers, who stood on the porch beside Anna. "You!" he accused. "You and your nutty ideas about animals. You did it.

What did you think? I was invading the bear's right to privacy, or something?"

Havemeyer took Jensen by the arm. "You're upset," he said. "Look, we'll get you to a doctor."

"I don't want a doctor. I want the police!"

"Mr. Jensen." Jupe stepped forward. "There could have been a second bear. We were here just after you shouted. There was a bear running away up the ski slope, and there was also the noise of something crashing through the trees over there."

"I was not hit by a bear!" insisted Jensen. He shot an angry look at Mr. Smathers.

"I am not in the habit of striking my fellow creatures," said Smathers primly. "Also, I could not possibly have struck you. I was in bed. Ask Mrs. Havemeyer. She was in the hall when I came out of my room."

Anna nodded. "That is right, Mr. Jensen. I heard a noise and put on my robe. I was at the top of the stairs when Mr. Smathers opened his door."

"It happened too fast," said Havemeyer soothingly. "You couldn't possibly remember it exactly. Not after being hit on the head."

"The neck," said Jensen stubbornly. "I got it in the neck. A rabbit punch. Since when do bears hand out rabbit punches?"

"Come in and we'll call the doctor," coaxed Havemeyer. He spoke as one would speak to an angry child.

"I don't want a doctor!" shouted Jensen. "Call the police. There's a criminal roaming around here assaulting innocent people."

"Innocent people should be in their beds at this hour of night," said Mr. Smathers, "not scaring the wits out of other creatures with their flash bulbs and their cameras."

"My camera!" Jensen lunged at the remains of his camera. "Oh, great!" He picked up two separate pieces and looked angrily at the loop of film that dangled from the wreckage. "Vandal!" accused Jensen. The remark seemed to be directed at Mr. Smathers.

"If you drop a camera, it will break," said Smathers. "And if you wish to call the police, I'll be happy to talk to them when they get here. In the meantime, I am going back to bed. Don't wake me unless there's a good reason."

Smathers marched into the inn, leaving Jensen to his rage.

"He's right," said Havemeyer reasonably. "We all ought to go back to bed." He turned to The Three Investigators. "Bring your sleeping bags inside," he told them. "You don't want to be out here with a bad bear on the loose."

"It wasn't a bear!" shouted Jensen.

"Then what was it?" demanded Havemeyer. "Jupe here heard something crashing through those trees, so unless someone from the village has suddenly taken to a life of crime, there had to be a second bear. Now, do you want us to call the doctor? If we call the sheriff, he'll only tell you not to wander around at night disturbing the wildlife."

That was true, and Jensen knew it. "All right, all right," he grumbled. "And I don't need a doctor." He went up the porch steps and into the kitchen, rubbing his neck.

Fifteen minutes later, The Three Investigators had moved their sleeping bags out of the tent and were comfortably installed in the living room of the inn. They waited until the noises on the second floor ceased. Then, in the darkness, Pete spoke.

"Jensen's lucky," he said. "Not too many people tangle with a bear and get off as easily as he did. Unless, of course, it really wasn't a bear."

Jupiter Jones frowned. "You're thinking the same thing that I'm thinking. Could a bear deliver a blow that would stun a man and still not leave a scratch on him? The skin on Jensen's neck wasn't broken."

"It couldn't have been anyone from the inn," said Bob. "Hans and Konrad don't hit people. Joe Havemeyer was in the office when it happened, and Cousin Anna and Mr. Smathers alibi each other. Even if he were a human fly and could walk up walls, Mr. Smathers couldn't have gotten back into his room so quickly that Cousin Anna saw him when she started downstairs."

"So it was either an outsider or a second bear," said Jupe. "In the morning, as soon as it's light, we'll go down to those trees south of the inn where the attacker ran after striking Mr. Jensen. It's been a dry year, but trees hold moisture and the earth there ought to be soft enough to show footprints. Whoever or whatever hit Jensen, he must have left tracks. We should be able to tell whether the attacker was a bear or a man."

5

The Missing Key

Jupiter Jones awakened to find Pete shaking his arm.
"We missed the boat," said Pete. "Get out of the sack
and see."

Jupe sat up. The room was still dim and gray.

"Joe Havemeyer beat us to it," reported Pete.

Next to Jupe, Bob turned over and stretched. "Beat
us to what?" he asked.

"We do not get to examine the backyard for bear
tracks or people tracks or any kind of tracks," Pete informed them. "Come and see. You wouldn't believe
me if I told you."

Bob and Jupe got up and followed Pete to the
kitchen. Pete went to the window near the range and
pointed out.

"How interesting," said Jupe.

"That's . . . that's crazy!" exclaimed Bob. He

scowled at Cousin Anna's husband, who was energetically sweeping the earth in the backyard with a broom.

"He's already swept the ground under the trees," said Pete. "He was finishing there when I woke you."

"Hmmm," mused Jupe. "Looks as if he's deliberately erasing any possible sign of Mr. Jensen's attacker. Very curious." He stepped to the door, opened it, and padded out onto the back porch in his stocking feet. "Good morning," he said brightly.

Havemeyer jumped slightly, then smiled. "Morning," he greeted Jupe. "Sleep okay after all the excitement?"

"Like a log," Jupiter assured him. "You're up early." Jupiter looked pointedly at the broom.

Havemeyer picked up the trash can which had been overturned and began to sweep the debris around the porch steps into a neat pile. "Got a lot to do," he told Jupe. "Want to get the trash all cleaned up or we'll have more bears roaming around here than you can shake a stick at. And after breakfast I'm going to work on the swimming pool. Go put your shoes on and I'll show you."

He deposited the trash in the can, then covered it and started up the porch steps.

Pete and Bob were standing innocently near the sink when Havemeyer and Jupe stepped into the kitchen.

"Morning," said Havemeyer. "Want to see my pool?"

The three boys got their shoes and followed Havemeyer to the excavation fifty feet behind the inn.

"I had a couple of men come up from Bishop with

heavy equipment to do the actual digging," said Havemeyer. "I'll put up the forms and pour the concrete myself, but I figured I'd be at it all year if I tried to dig it myself."

"I see what you mean," said Pete. "That must be ten feet deep!"

"Twelve," said Havemeyer.

"But," said Pete, "there's no shallow end."

"That's right," Havemeyer said.

Pete frowned. "I never saw a pool like this. If you don't have a shallow part, what about the people who can't swim and just like to go in and bob around?"

"I see you get the idea," said Havemeyer. "People who can't swim won't be able to use the pool. I once saw a man who couldn't swim lose his footing in a pool. It wasn't funny."

"Oh," said Pete.

Hans and Konrad hallooed cheerfully from the house.

"We're out here," called Havemeyer.

The brothers came hurrying down the steps and across the yard. "Ho!" said Hans, when he caught sight of Havemeyer's excavation. "Swimming pool, huh?" He had the air of one who is determined to be pleasant.

"The swimming pool," said Havemeyer.

"You are making it yourself?" asked Konrad.

Havemeyer nodded. "It'll keep me out from under Anna's feet for a while."

"Making a pool is hard work," said Hans. "We have a holiday. We will help."

"Oh, no, no, no!" said Havemeyer quickly. "You're on your vacation. I wouldn't think of having you . . ."

"What better thing can we do with our vacation than help our cousin's husband?" said Konrad. The words were friendly enough, but Konrad's voice was very firm, as if he would not stand for any argument.

Havemeyer shrugged and began to explain his plans for the pool to the brothers. The Three Investigators wandered back toward the inn.

"Hans and Konrad have just earned the right to stay here," murmured Jupe. "Helping with the pool will give them an excuse to stick around and find out more about Joe Havemeyer."

"I'm not sure his head is screwed on the right way," declared Pete. "I mean, I never saw a swimming pool that didn't have a shallow end."

Breakfast that morning was a tense meal. Mr. Jensen spoke to no one, and he avoided even looking at Mr. Smathers. Mr. Smathers openly disapproved of eating eggs and was horrified when Cousin Anna carried in a platter of sausages. Cousin Anna herself ate almost nothing. She sat and twisted the wedding ring on her finger, urging everyone to have second helpings. Havemeyer refused, and he and Hans and Konrad went out to the backyard to start work on the pool. Mr. Smathers took a muffin, stuffed it in his shirt pocket, and went out and down the road toward the campground. Mr. Jensen said a rather sullen thank you to Anna and announced that he had business in Bishop.

Cousin Anna looked sadly at the leftover food. "I think no one was very hungry," she said to the boys.

"Everything was very good," said Jupiter quickly. "In fact, you remind me of my Aunt Mathilda."

"Aunt Mathilda?" Anna said. "Oh, yes. The lady who has been so kind to Hans and Konrad."

"She's a great cook, too," Jupiter told her.

Pete chuckled. "That accounts for Jupe's heft."

"Aunt Mathilda and I are going on a diet," said Jupe, "as soon as I get back to Rocky Beach."

Bob laughed. "I've heard that before. I'll believe it when I see it, Baby Fatso."

"All right! All right!" Jupe was so nettled that he almost shouted.

"Baby Fatso?" said Anna. "I think I have heard that name before."

"If you watch the late, late, late show on television, you may catch Jupe. He was a child star—practically an American institution."

"Oh, yes. Hans and Konrad did not write to me about that." Anna brightened suddenly. "They write always that you are clever boys and can find out about things."

"You saw our card," said Jupe stiffly. He was still smarting slightly after the rebuff of the day before.

"The card? Yes, and I think I have been very foolish. I have looked everywhere and I cannot find my key. It is very important. Perhaps you will find it for me."

"You wish to retain The Three Investigators?" asked Jupe.

"Retain? What is this retain?"

"Jupe only means that you authorize us to search for the missing key," Bob explained. "Sometimes there is a fee for our services, but not in this case. We *are* free-loading here, and the food is delicious."

"Way ahead of that canned stuff we brought when we thought we'd be staying in the campground," said Pete.

"Thank you." Anna smiled. "Retain. Yes, I wish to retain you to find the key. It is so silly. You see, when I left here to go to Lake Tahoe, I did not wish to carry the key with me, so I hid it in some clever place. Now I do not remember where I put it. I was so clever that I fooled myself."

"What does the key look like?" asked Jupiter.

"It is small," said Anna. "Like this." She held up her hand with thumb and forefinger about two inches apart. "It is the key to my safe deposit box."

"I can see why that's important," said Pete, "but couldn't you go to the bank and explain that you lost the key? They'd give you a duplicate, wouldn't they?"

"My father lost the key to his safe deposit box," said Bob. "He didn't have any trouble about it. Oh, he did have to see an officer at the bank, and I think they had to change the lock on his box. There was a fee for that, but not very much."

"I am embarrassed," said Anna. "At the bank in Bishop they have much respect for me. They know I am careful, and when I needed money to buy the ski lift, they lent it to me. I do not wish to go to the bank and say I have been so foolish that I lost such an important thing."

"Very well," said Jupiter. "The Three Investigators should be able to save you that embarrassment. It can't

be an impossible task. The inn isn't large. Where did
you usually keep the key, by the way?"

"In the drawer of my desk. But now . . ." Anna
spread her hands in a gesture of despair. "I remember
thinking that my inn would be empty, and I would
hide the key in case someone breaks in. But I cannot
remember where."

"So we search," said Pete. He pushed back his chair
and got up from the table.

"Shall we start with the office?" asked Jupiter.

"We have already looked in the office," Anna told
him. "It is not there."

"We can look again." Jupe's round face assumed a
hopeful expression. "We might think of something you
missed."

"If you like." Anna began to clear the table.

The Three Investigators went immediately to the
office, which was still a jumble of papers, folders, and
ledgers.

"I think we're wasting our time here, Jupe," said
Pete. "Cousin Anna and her husband have really
turned this place upside down. They'd have found a
pin if it had been lost here."

"I agree." Jupe sat down at the desk. From the
kitchen came the clatter of dishes and the rushing
sound of water filling the sink. "But we may discover
what Anna's husband was doing in here last night
when everyone else was in bed. Hans and Konrad have
asked us to find out all we can about Havemeyer. So
first we'll find out what interests him so much in this
office."

Jupe began leafing through a stack of papers on the desk. "Hm. A letter from Hans, and another from Konrad. This one's over two years old. Anna must have saved all the letters her cousins sent her."

"No reason for Havemeyer to sit up all night reading them, is there?" Bob took a ledger from the stack on the bookcase and began to page through it. "Hans and Konrad are here now, in the flesh, and if he wants to know anything about them he can just ask."

"No reason at all." Jupe leaned on his elbows and began to pull at his lower lip, a sure sign that he was concentrating intensely.

"Say, here's something," said Bob. He thrust a ledger across the desk to Jupiter. "Cousin Anna's record of her savings."

"That's a pretty hefty bankbook," observed Pete.

"It's not a bankbook at all. It's only a record book. There's a column for money put in, and one for money taken out, and the last column on each page is for money that's available."

Jupiter flipped the pages until he was halfway through the ledger. Then he stopped. "The latest entry is for the week before last," he told Bob and Pete. "The week before last, Anna put 175 dollars wherever she puts her money. She took nothing out, and the last column indicates that she has 10,823 dollars available."

"Wow!" cried Pete. "If that's in cash, Cousin Anna is way ahead of about ninety percent of the American public. I learned that in social studies this year. Most people never have cash, and they're so far in debt that a flat tire can be a real emergency."

"So Cousin Anna is very well off," said Jupe. "Bob, we'd better find her key as quickly as possible, and then get to a telephone in the village and call your father. I'd be very interested to know if the credit bureau in Reno has a file on Havemeyer."

"You think he could be planning to get his mitts on Cousin Anna's loot?" asked Pete.

"It's possible. Certainly Hans and Konrad suspect this, and it's easy to see that Hans and Konrad make him uncomfortable. He was not pleased when they decided to spend their vacation here helping with the pool. And that doesn't make sense. The pool itself doesn't make sense. Sweeping the yard doesn't make sense. A tranquilizer gun doesn't make sense."

Jupe held up a warning hand at the sound of footsteps in the living room. A few seconds later, Anna appeared at the door of the office. "Well?" she said.

"You were right," Jupiter told her. "The key isn't here."

"We'll search the rest of the inn," Bob assured her. "Will Mr. Jensen and Mr. Smathers mind if we look in their rooms? Would you hide the key in a guest room?"

"Perhaps," said Anna. "I had no guests when I left for my wedding. But do not touch the luggage. It is not necessary, and they would be very angry if you touched their things."

"Of course not." Jupe stood up. "Would you like us to straighten this room for you?"

"It is better if I do it," said Anna. "You will not know where things belong."

"Very well." Jupe came out from behind the desk.

He was almost at the door when he stopped, struck by a sudden thought. "Have you used your checkbook lately?" he asked Anna. "I didn't see a checkbook here."

"I do not have a checkbook," Anna told him. "I always pay for things with cash."

"Everything?" Jupe was astounded. "Isn't it dangerous to keep a lot of cash here?"

"I do not keep much cash here," said Anna. "I keep my money in the bank, in the safe deposit box. You see, that is why the key is so important. Soon I must pay my bills. I will need money. Also, my husband has ordered cement for the swimming pool. I wish to pay for that when it is delivered."

"In cash?" asked Jupe.

"It is safer," declared Cousin Anna. "If I have a checkbook, someone can steal my checks and sign my name. Someone can take all I have before I even know. If I have real money, I do not keep more than I need and no one steals it. I put it under my pillow at night. In the daytime, I have it with me."

"I don't think the police would approve of your system, Mrs. Havemeyer," said Jupiter. "If you pay cash for everything, people must know that you have large sums here from time to time. Suppose someone held you up?"

Cousin Anna smiled. "I think my husband would shoot someone who did that," she said.

"You know," said Pete, "I think he would!"

6

Monster Mountain

The Three Investigators devoted the rest of the morning to a painstaking search of the inn. They turned back rugs and peeked under bureaus and felt along the tops of window frames and doorways. Pete got up on a chair and took all the dishes down from the top shelves in the kitchen. Bob shook each jar, upended every cup, and probed the flour cannister and the sugar bowl with a long spoon. Jupe scanned every rafter on the second floor of the inn, and then went down into the basement to poke in cracks and corners in the cement walls. Anna's shoes were taken out of the closet and examined. Her coat pockets were searched and her handbags were turned out.

"Are you sure it's here?" asked Jupe, when he and Bob and Pete assembled for lunch. "Are you sure you didn't drop it someplace—perhaps at the bank the last time you used it?"

Anna was sure.

Pete slumped at the table. "Beats me," he said. "We've gone over every inch of this place. How could you hide anything that well and not remember where you hid it? That takes genius!"

Anna sighed and put a platter of grilled cheese sandwiches on the table. "Perhaps you should rest and look again tomorrow," she suggested. "I will try to remember. But I try and try, and I cannot remember."

"Don't try," advised Jupiter. "Don't even think about it and it may come to you."

Anna did not join the boys for lunch. Instead, she went into her office and closed the door.

"Why is she that upset?" said Bob. "She can get another key, or another lock, or whatever she needs to get into her safe deposit box."

Jupe could only shrug, and the boys ate in silence. They hastily washed their dishes, then went out into the backyard. Jupe paused and stared at the clean-swept earth, which now showed the footprints of everyone who had gone back and forth from the pool site.

"Ho, Jupe!"

Hans was calling from the edge of Joe Havemeyer's excavation. The boys heard a vigorous pounding. Someone was hammering at the bottom of the future swimming pool.

Jupe, Pete, and Bob hurried over and looked down. Konrad was in the hole, pounding nails into planks to make the forms that would hold the poured concrete.

"Did you find out anything?" asked Hans.

Konrad stopped hammering and waited.

"We've been looking for Cousin Anna's key," said Jupe. "I'm afraid we didn't find it. Now we can concentrate on Havemeyer. I'm sure we'll be able to get some information about him for you. Bob has to make a telephone call. Where is Havemeyer, by the way?"

Hans pointed toward the top of the ski slope. "He has taken his gun and some things in a knapsack and has gone up there. He said he had work to do in the high meadow and he will come back later."

The Three Investigators left the brothers and walked down the drive. They turned right on the village street, and soon came to the little gas station where Hans and Konrad had asked for directions the day before. The inquisitive attendant was nowhere to be seen, and the place appeared to be closed. There was a telephone booth on one corner of the property. Bob stepped inside, closed the door, and placed a call to his father at the newspaper office.

"Well?" said Pete, when Bob emerged from the phone booth.

"We're in luck," Bob reported. "I got the standard lecture about calling him when he's at work, but he does know a newspaperman who lives in Reno, and he'll get in touch with him and see what he can find out about Havemeyer. He said I should call him tomorrow night after he's home."

"Good enough," said Jupiter.

The boys strolled back up the village street past the Slalom Inn, then went on down the road toward the Sky Village Campground.

"This vacation isn't exactly what I expected," said Pete. "We were going to camp out and hike and fish. Instead we wind up sleeping on the floor in the inn and eating Cousin Anna's home cooking. If it were a little foggy, I'd think we were back in Rocky Beach."

"We can camp out, I suppose," said Bob. "We could move our tent down here this afternoon. Hans and Konrad probably wouldn't come. They're too nervous about Cousin Anna's husband. But we can do it."

Jupe grinned. "Aren't you afraid of the bears?" he asked.

"That bear didn't bother us last night," Bob pointed out. "He was only after food."

"But something bothered Mr. Jensen," Jupe reminded him. "What could it have been? And why did Havemeyer sweep away the tracks this morning?"

The three boys went around a bend in the road and the campground lay before them. It consisted of five stone firepits in the ground, and an equal number of redwood picnic tables. To the right was the bed of a small stream. It was almost dry. Only a trickle of water ran down through the rocks. Beyond the campground a path twisted away through the brush.

Pete looked at the creek and ran his hand through his hair. "I can see what Joe Havemeyer meant about water being a problem here," he said. "If we move our gear down, we'll have to bring water from the inn."

"There doesn't seem to be much point to that," said

Jupiter. "Besides, I'd like to stay close to the inn, at least until we get more information about Havemeyer. There are too many odd things about him. And the attack on Mr. Jensen . . ."

"That couldn't have been Havemeyer," said Bob. "We could see Havemeyer inside the inn at the time Jensen was hit."

"No. It couldn't have been Havemeyer. But something fishy is going on at the inn. I'd like to know what it is."

There was a rustling in the bushes behind Jupe. All three boys jumped.

"Scare you?" asked an amused voice. "Sorry about that."

Jupe spun around. The man who ran the gas station in Sky Village emerged from a clump of wild lilac. He was busily stuffing a wad of muddy, crumpled paper into a burlap sack.

"You boys a little bear-shy?" he asked. His keen eyes twinkled. "Hear you had a scare at the inn last night."

"How . . . how did you know?" asked Jupe.

"Mr. Jensen stopped by this morning to buy some gas," explained the man. "I noticed he had a stiff neck, so I asked what was the matter. I kind of like to find out about people. He was madder 'n a hornet. Claimed somebody gave him a rabbit punch while he was trying to take a picture of a bear."

"So far as we know, that's what happened," said Bob. "Mr. Havemeyer thinks it was a second bear."

"Interesting way for a bear to behave," said the man. "Still, you can't tell, and we've had a lot of bears in the village this year. Always do in the dry years. They raid everybody's trash cans. I always let them alone. That way I don't have any grief."

The man surveyed the campground. "That's better," he announced. "A couple came in here from the city last week and made an awful mess. Paper towels all over creation and orange peels in the creek. Makes you lose your faith in people."

"Are you responsible for the campground?" asked Bob.

"Not really," said the man, "but it's about the only thing around here that brings in business in the summer, and I like to sell gas. Campers tell one another about the conditions in the different campgrounds. If this place got a bad name, I could close up my station and starve from May until the snow flies."

"I see," said Bob.

"My name's Richardson, by the way," said the man. "Charlie Richardson, only they call me Gabby." He chuckled. "I wonder why they do that."

Pete laughed. "I wonder, too," he said. He held out his hand. "I'm Pete Crenshaw and this is Jupiter Jones. My pal with the glasses is Bob Andrews."

Gabby Richardson said he was pleased to meet the boys, and shook hands all around.

"You thinking of moving your camp down here?" he asked. "I saw when I passed Anna's place that you had your tent out under the trees."

"Actually, we slept inside last night," said Jupe. "After the bears raided the trash, Mr. Havemeyer thought it would be better."

Gabby Richardson laughed. "Easy knowing Anna Schmid's new husband hasn't been on Monster Mountain very long if he's spooked by a bear or two."

"Monster Mountain?" echoed Pete.

"Yep. Oh, I guess for the benefit of you tourists I ought to call it Mount Lofty, like it says on the maps. But when I was a kid, there were just five families living here, and we called it Monster Mountain." He pointed toward a watchtower which was barely visible on the high slopes toward the north. "See that fire tower? It's abandoned now, but when it was used it was officially the Monster Mountain tower."

Pete sat down at one of the picnic tables. "Any reason why they called it that?" he asked.

Gabby Richardson sat next to Pete and leaned back against the table. "When I was young," he said, "the grown folks used to tell us there were monsters on the mountain—giants and ogres who lived in caves and ate kids who stayed out past dark."

Bob laughed. "That sounds like a story some mother made up to keep her kids in line."

"Probably," agreed Richardson, "but we believed every word of it, and what the grownups didn't tell us, we made up ourselves. We scared each other half to death telling how terrible creatures came out on nights when there was a full moon and prowled around houses, looking for ways to get in. An old trapper lived here once, and he swore he'd found the footprints of some huge man in the snow high up near the glacier. Said it was a barefoot man. That was pretty silly. A man would freeze his toes off running barefoot up there."

"Sounds like you had fun being scared," said Pete.

"Oh, we had fun, all right, but we didn't stay out after dark, you can bet. Funny. You'd almost think the hermit knew those stories and they worked on his mind, but he didn't."

"A hermit?" Bob sat down on a boulder near the picnic table. "First monsters and then a hermit. You had a colorful childhood."

"Oh, the hermit wasn't around when I was a kid," said Richardson. "He wandered in here three . . . no, it was four years ago. He climbed on foot from Bishop with a pack on his back—a young man, maybe twenty-five or thirty. It was summer when he came and there weren't too many people around, so when I saw him standing in the middle of the street looking kind of bewildered, I asked him what he wanted. He said he wanted a good place to meditate. I told him we didn't have a church here in Sky Village, but that wasn't what he had in mind. He wanted a place where he could just sit and let his spirit blend into the universe.

"That sounded like a harmless thing to do, so I told him he might try the meadow up above the ski slope. Hardly anyone goes there in the summer. I figured he'd go there for an afternoon and sit in the grass and think a bit, but I was wrong. Darned if he didn't go up the mountain and build himself a little shack. He bought lumber and tar paper and a few nails in the village, but never any food. Guess he lived on berries, like the bears, or acorns, like the squirrels."

"Back to nature, huh?" said Bob. "What happened to him?"

"Well," said Gabby Richardson, "I personally think it addles a man's brains to be alone all that much. That young hermit didn't talk to anybody, and if anyone went up the mountain, he'd shut himself up in his shack. He lasted it out about three months. Then one day he came down and went through the village like a shot. I didn't see him, but Jeff, who boxes things over at the market when it's open, said he was yelling about a monster in the meadow. Last Jeff saw, that hermit was making tracks down the road to Bishop."

In spite of himself, Pete shivered. "You never saw him again?" he asked.

"Not hide nor hair," said Richardson.

Jupiter Jones looked up at the peaks towering above them. "Monsters," he said. "I wonder . . ."

Richardson snorted and sat up straight. "Don't pay too much mind to that story," he said. "The boy got to seeing things up there all by himself. Anybody would. It isn't healthy for a man to be so alone." He stood up. "If you want to camp out here, camp out. Don't worry about monsters, and the bears won't give you trouble if you don't give them trouble. Just don't leave food around."

He threw his burlap sack over one shoulder and started toward the road that led back to Sky Village. At the edge of the campground he stopped and turned back to warn, "And don't litter!"

"We won't," promised Bob.

The gas station attendant tramped up the road. In a few minutes he was out of sight.

"Monster Mountain," said Bob. "Those had to be stories the grownups told the kids to keep them in line. There couldn't have been monsters here. The Sierras aren't the Himalayas. Why, there've been pack trains and tourists and campers ever since—"

"Not everywhere," interrupted Jupiter. "This range covers a vast area. There must be many places where the hikers and campers can't go."

Pete shuddered. "Jupe, you give me the creeps. Don't tell me you think that hermit really saw a monster."

"Even the most fantastic stories usually have a grain of truth in them somewhere," said Jupiter Jones. "Unless Mr. Gabby Richardson made that entire tale up out of thin air, we can assume that there was a hermit and that he saw something that frightened him and—"

"Listen!" Bob was suddenly tense. He looked around toward the creek. "Someone's there!"

The bushes on the far side of the creek rustled softly and, though the afternoon was still, the boys could see branches moving.

Pete stood like a statue, eyes glues to the clump of shrubs beyond the stream. He thought he saw a strange shadow in their midst.

The rustling grew louder, nearer.

"Something's there," whispered Bob, "and it's coming this way!"

7

The Animal Man

Closer and closer came the soft rustlings in the brush.

The Three Investigators broke out in a cold sweat. Visions of strange creatures seized their minds . . . ogres and giants prowling through the forest . . . formless monsters sending a hermit screaming down the mountain . . . sinister shapes lurking in the shadows on moonlit nights . . .

Crackle. Rustle. Crunch.

Closer and closer . . .

Suddenly the noises stopped. The bushes across the creek were still. The silence was dreadful. Would the thing attack or not?

Then: "Well, now! Sorry, friend," said a familiar voice. "I almost stepped on you."

Pete hadn't realized that he was holding his breath.

He gasped, then began breathing quickly, drawing the thin, sweet mountain air into his lungs in gulps.

"It's Mr. Smathers!" choked out Jupiter Jones. His throat had gone dry with fright. He slumped back against the picnic table. "What a relief!"

Bob's laugh had an edge of hysteria. "Did you think it was the monster of Monster Mountain? For a second, I did."

"The power of suggestion," said Jupe. "We listen to a weird story, and then are scared half to death by the first person to wander along." He raised his voice and called, "Mr. Smathers?"

The bushes beyond the creek parted and Mr. Smathers' thin face peered out at the boys. The weedy little man was wearing a canvas hat with a small brim, and he seemed unaware of the fact that his nose was sunburned and that he had a scratch across his forehead. "You're disturbing the peace," he said. His voice was stern, but the corners of his mouth crinkled in a smile.

"You scared us," said Pete. "We thought you were a bear, at the very least."

"I wouldn't mind being a bear this afternoon," declared Smathers. "I found a bee tree. What a feast for a bear!" He stepped out of the bushes and stood at the edge of the creek. The boys saw that he was holding a skunk in one arm, very gently, as a mother might hold a child.

"Good golly!" exclaimed Pete.

Smathers' eyes went to the little black-and-white animal. "Handsome, isn't she?" he said.

"Mr. Smathers!" Bob said frantically. "Put it down!"

Smathers laughed. "Does my friend upset you?" He stroked the skunk under the chin with his forefinger. "Isn't that silly?" he said to the animal. "The boys are afraid you'll turn your scent glands on them. You wouldn't do that, would you? Not unless you had to."

Smathers put the skunk down. "Better get along," he advised the creature. "Not everyone understands you like I do."

The skunk waddled a few steps, then stopped and looked around as if questioning Smathers.

"Go on," urged Smathers. "I want to have a few words with our young friends here and you make them nervous. Oh, I am sorry that I disturbed you while you were having your nap. Clumsy of me. I won't do it again, I promise."

The skunk seemed satisfied with this. It disappeared into the bushes, and Mr. Smathers climbed down the bank into the creek bed and crossed the trickle of water.

"Charming creatures, skunks," said Smathers, as he joined Jupiter, Pete, and Bob in the campground. "One shouldn't really have favorites, I suppose, but I think I enjoy skunks almost more than any other animal."

"If I hadn't seen that, I wouldn't believe it," declared Bob.

Pete frowned furiously. "It's a trick," he decided. "That just has to be somebody's pet skunk. It must have had its scent glands removed."

"What a dreadful idea!" exclaimed Mr. Smathers.

"Absolutely barbarous! Oh, I know that people do make house pets of skunks and remove the scent glands. And what happens then?"

"Nothing," said Pete. "Nothing happens. That's why the scent glands are removed—so that nothing can happen."

"Typical human reasoning," said Smathers. "You take an animal that has been provided by nature with a perfect defense system and remove that system. The animal becomes helpless—completely dependent on the human since it can't defend itself. Then the human proudly says that he owns the animal, as if one creature could own another. Perfectly dreadful!"

The boys were silent, a bit startled by the violence of Mr. Smathers' tone.

"Now," said Smathers, after a moment, "if people would only use their brains and take the time to understand their fellow creatures, there wouldn't be any need for that sort of savagery. We could all go into the wilderness, provided we minded our manners, and we could visit with our wild friends there. We would have the decency to permit them their freedom."

Mr. Smathers took a paper sack out of his pocket and poured a few peanuts out of it into the palm of his hand. "Be still and I'll show you," he told the boys.

He pursed his lips and let out a chirruping sound.

A blue jay wheeled overhead, circled the campground once, and lighted at Smathers' feet. The bird ignored the boys and screeched once at Smathers.

"Not so fast," said Smathers. "Wait for the others."

The jay scolded him.

"It won't be long," Smathers told the bird. "Have a little patience, if you please."

A ground squirrel appeared and scampered to Smathers. The jay shrieked impatiently at the squirrel, and the squirrel chattered back in an irritated way.

"Don't quarrel," said Smathers. "There's plenty for everyone."

The squirrel stopped chattering and began to rub its face with its forepaws in an embarrassed fashion.

Two chipmunks darted across the clearing, almost scampering over Pete's toes.

"Ah, there you are at last!" said Smathers. "All right. We can begin."

The squirrel waited while Smathers held out the nuts to the jay. The jay snapped up two nuts, then hopped a foot or two away while Smathers fed the squirrel. Then the chipmunks took their turn.

"You see," said Smathers to the boys, "they will give way to one another if only you explain things to them properly. No shoving. No snatching."

The boys didn't speak, but Jupe nodded.

When the chipmunks had munched the last of the nuts, Smathers dismissed the animals much as a school-master might dismiss a class. The jay flew to the top of a big pine, lighted there for a second, and squawked loudly. Then it flew away. The squirrel ran to hide under a heap of stones on the bank of the creek, and the chipmunks scampered off into the trees.

"I'm spoiling them, of course," said Smathers. "But then, every creature can use a little spoiling once in a while."

"Yes, you are spoiling them," said Jupe. "In the national parks the rangers always warn visitors not to feed the animals. They forget how to find their own food if too many people give them nuts and popcorn and things like that."

"That's why I hate to go to the national parks," snapped Mr. Smathers. "Stupid people line up everywhere with their hands full of civilized trash that they shove at the wild things, and the animals gorge themselves. Then, when winter comes, the people go home and don't worry for a second about the harm they've done, and a lot of the animals starve. That's murder, just as surely as shooting a deer with a rifle is murder. I only bring a few nuts to my friends, and I've warned the squirrel and those chipmunks about taking food from strangers. They understand what can happen. They know that I'm only giving them a little treat. It's much the same as buying an ice-cream cone for a favorite nephew."

"I see," said Bob. "You've explained to the animals that they've got to watch out for people. And you figure they understand?"

"I know that they understand," declared Smathers. "They've told me. Oh, I'm not sure about that jay. He's a greedy one. He may not understand much of anything except filling his craw. Still, he's beautiful to look at, don't you think?"

"Very," said Jupiter Jones.

"Fortunately for him, he's not a member of a rare species," said Smathers, "or there'd be madmen out

here hunting him so they could put him in a zoo. Now there's cruelty for you—a zoo!"

Mr. Smathers' face took on a reddish tinge, and his lips clamped together angrily.

"I read somewhere that animals live longer in zoos," said Pete softly.

"Live longer? Well, maybe they do, if you can call it living. They're either caged or stranded in the bottom of a pit. If they're big, the keepers are afraid of them so they get stunned with tranquilizers if they need any attention. You call that living?"

"I guess I wouldn't like it," admitted Pete.

"You know you wouldn't like it." Mr. Smathers' watery eyes narrowed. "Tranquilizers!" he said. "I know why that lout at the inn has a tranquilizer gun, but he won't use it, not as long as I've got breath in my body!"

"Why *does* Mr. Havemeyer have a tranquilizer gun?" asked Jupiter Jones.

"Eh?" Smathers glared at Jupe as if Jupe were an enemy. "I won't tell you," he said. "If I told you, you might believe me and that would be a tragedy."

He stamped away, out of the campground and up the road toward the inn.

"Now what did he mean by that?" said Bob. "If we believed him, it would be a tragedy. Why?"

"Havemeyer must want to capture something," said Jupe slowly. "The only reason for a tranquilizer gun is to shoot an animal without killing it. Does he want to capture a bear? I think not. We'd find that easy enough to believe. No, Smathers is talking about an animal we might not believe in. Now what sort of creature is that?"

He stopped, as if reluctant to voice his thoughts, and looked at the others with wonder.

8

Joe Havemeyer's Vision

The Three Investigators had almost reached the inn when a truck came slowly up the village road, gears grinding as the driver shifted down to make the grade.

"That must be the cement for the swimming pool," said Pete.

The truck turned into the driveway of the inn and made its way past the parking lot and into the back-yard. The truck driver got out of the cab. He and Joe Havemeyer began to unload sacks of cement and sand, piling them on wooden skids near the excavation for the pool. Hans and Konrad were not in sight.

"That's a lot of cement," Bob observed.

"It's a big swimming pool," said Pete. "Big and deep. I wonder if Cousin Anna knew the cement was coming today. She said she wanted to pay for it when it was delivered, and we haven't found her safe deposit key."

"If her reputation is so good, I am sure she'll be able to sign for the cement," Jupiter pointed out. "Or her husband might pay for it. He's the one who is so enthusiastic about the pool."

The boys went up the front steps and into the inn. The big living room was empty, but from upstairs came the voices of Hans and Konrad.

"Anna!" It was Joe Havemeyer, shouting from the backyard. "Anna, can you come out here for a second?"

Anna's firm step sounded in the kitchen. The back door opened and then closed. Jupiter, Pete, and Bob drifted through the living room and into the kitchen, where the window above the sink was open. They looked through the window and saw Anna approach Havemeyer and the truck driver. She was wearing an apron, and she wiped her hands on a dish towel as she walked.

"Is it everything you need?" she asked her husband.

Havemeyer nodded. "I'm all set for now," he said.

"Good." Anna took a paper from the truck driver and examined it. "It is right?" she asked Havemeyer.

"I checked it," he told her. "The bill's correct."

"Good." She turned to the truck driver. "I do not have the money here today," she told him. "It is all right with your boss if I pay for the cement next week?"

"Oh, sure, Miss Schmid," said the man.

"Mrs. Havemeyer," Anna corrected him.

"Sorry, Mrs. Havemeyer. If you'll just sign the bill so we have a record that you received the cement, we can—"

"Sign the bill?" For the first time, Anna seemed a bit uncertain. Her whole body had gone tense.

"It's a rule," said the driver. "If we don't get the money, we get a signature."

"Oh," said Anna. "All right. I'll take it in the house and sign."

"No need to go to all that trouble." The driver took a ball-point pen from his shirt pocket and handed it to Anna. "Here. Just sign anywhere on the bill. Want to lean on the fender?"

"Oh." Anna looked at her husband, then back at the driver. She handed the dish towel to her husband and put the bill on the fender of the truck. With the driver's pen she wrote something on the bill. It seemed to the boys in the kitchen that she was a long time about it. When she finished, she handed the bill and the pen to the driver. "That is all right?" she asked.

The man barely glanced at the bill. "That's fine, Mrs. Havemeyer."

"Usually I write more neatly," said Anna. "Today I am baking bread, working with the dough. My hand shakes."

"We all have our shaky days," said the driver cheerfully. He folded the bill and tucked it into his pocket, climbed into the truck, and backed out into the road.

"Idiot!" snapped Havemeyer when the truck was gone.

"I told you I did not want to do that," said Anna. "You could have signed."

"It's Anna Schmid who's the old customer with the building supply people, not Joe Havemeyer," he said. "You didn't have to run off at the mouth to that driver. He's not a penmanship teacher." Havemeyer was silent for a second, then repeated, "Idiot!"

Anna whirled around and started back toward the house. She had gone only a few steps when she stopped. "You are the idiot," she said to Havemeyer. Her voice was low and very intense. "You and that stupid hole in the ground. I think you see things that are not real."

"It's real, all right," declared Havemeyer. "I saw it up on the meadow and it's been down here."

"I do not believe it," said Anna.

"You don't believe anything you can't taste or touch or count and put in a bank," declared Havemeyer. "You're a plodder. You wouldn't know an original idea if it came up and bit you on the lip. Without me—"

"I know. I know. I know all about that. You have the vision, hah? You have the imagination? Without you, where would I be? I think without you I would be better off. I am the one who takes the risk, and you are safe, you and your vision."

"You'll see," said Havemeyer.

"I had better," Anna snapped. She started again for the kitchen door.

"Cheese it!" whispered Pete.

The Three Investigators retreated from the kitchen to the living room and arranged themselves hastily in chairs. A moment later Anna stomped into the room, then stopped abruptly when she saw the boys.

"Oh," she said. "I did not know you were back."

Jupiter put down the magazine he was pretending to read and stood up. "We were down at the campground this afternoon," he told Cousin Anna. "We had an interesting talk with Mr. Smathers."

Anna nodded. "He is a strange little man," she said.

"He claims he can talk with animals and they understand him."

Anna shrugged. "Men!" she said. "Their heads are filled with cotton—all of them." She went past the boys and up the stairs, and the boys heard the sound of a door slamming.

"I think," said Bob, "that the honeymoon is over."

Pete scratched his ear and frowned. "I don't get it," he said. "She didn't want to sign for that cement and she lied to the driver. She's not baking bread. And what risk is she talking about?"

Jupiter Jones leaned against the fireplace. "Cousin Anna thinks her new husband is seeing things. She doesn't believe it's real—something Havemeyer saw up in the meadow, something that's been down here."

Pete got up and began to pace back and forth, his shoulders hunched and his head down. "Could it be," he asked, "that there is some truth in Gabby Richardson's stories?"

"A tranquilizer gun," said Jupiter. "A tranquilizer gun and something Havemeyer saw up on the meadow. Fellows, I think we know why Havemeyer has that gun!"

There was dead silence for perhaps half a minute, then Bob said softly, "He's hunting a monster."

"That's . . . that's wild!" said Pete.

"Utterly insane," agreed Jupiter, "but I think that must be what he's doing. Now listen, we're on vacation. Why don't we go for a hike up on the meadow tomorrow?"

"A hike or a monster hunt?" asked Pete.

"A tracking expedition," said Jupe. "If there is something strange wandering around up there, we should be able to find traces. There should be tracks."

Pete looked rather pale. "Maybe it isn't the kind of thing that leaves tracks," he said.

"Certainly it leaves tracks," declared Jupiter. "Joe Havemeyer swept the yard this morning so that no one could see its tracks. It isn't a bear—there's nothing special about a bear—so it's something else."

Jupe grinned. "Mr. Smathers knows what it is, but he'll never tell. But for the first time that swimming pool makes sense. I know what that hole in the ground reminds me of—one of the animal pits at the San Diego Zoo!"

9

The Beast in the Woods

The Three Investigators were up at daybreak the next morning. They rolled up their sleeping bags and stowed them in the closet under the stairs, then left a note on the kitchen table to inform Hans and Konrad that they were going on a hike. After a quick breakfast of toast and milk, they were out of the inn and working their way up toward the higher country beyond the ski slope. Jupe carried a knapsack, and Pete had a canteen of water slung from his belt.

At first the boys climbed in the cleared area of the ski slope, but the loose stones kept rolling under their feet. After Bob had stumbled twice, they took to the firmer ground under the trees that grew alongside the slope. There they made better time.

After twenty minutes, even Pete was panting for breath in the thin air. He stopped climbing and leaned against a tree trunk. "From the inn, this mountain didn't look awfully high," he gasped.

Bob laughed. "Is the great athlete out of condition?"

"My lungs are spoiled," said Pete. "They're used to operating at sea level."

Jupiter stood still and breathed in and out for a second or two. "It shouldn't be very far now," he decided.

"Keep telling yourself that," said Pete.

Jupe nodded and the boys climbed on, sometimes pulling themselves up by grasping tree limbs. It was another ten minutes before the ground under their feet was level. The trees grew more sparsely. Then they were out from under the pines and standing at the edge of a mountain meadow.

"Beautiful!" gasped Jupiter, when he got his breath.

The wind made ripples on the long, green grass, and here and there a boulder thrust up, sun-bleached and white. Huge trees rimmed the meadow on three sides. On the fourth side, the side which ended at the top of the ski slope, the boys could see for miles. The towers of the ski lift marched down the slope from the meadow to the road and Anna's inn, far below. Beyond the inn were stands of pine, and way beyond that, the dry, sandy stretches of the Owens Valley. Behind the boys, to the west, rose the rocky summit of Mount Lofty, flanked by other, higher peaks of the Sierras. On some of the mountaintops were glaciers which never melted, even in midsummer.

The boys walked slowly along until Bob spotted a track in the bare earth near the rim of the ski slope. He pulled out a paperback wildlife manual that he'd found at the inn, and turned to the chapter on animal tracks. Kneeling down, he compared the print in the earth with the drawing of a bear track in the book, then shrugged. "It's a bear, all right," he told Jupe and Pete. "That's exactly what you would expect to find up here."

"It isn't what we're looking for," said Jupiter.

"What *are* we looking for?" asked Pete. "Also, do we really want to find it?"

"Something different," declared Jupe. "Some kind of track that isn't in that manual."

"I hope we only find the track," said Pete. "Not the thing that made it."

The wind gusted across the meadow, rustling the grass and making the trees whisper. Suddenly, from behind the boys, there came a soft, inquisitive whimper.

Pete jumped.

Jupiter Jones turned. "Oh, no!" he said.

Pete heard something scamper and he felt a sniffing at his ankle. He looked down. A bear cub, only a few months old, stared up at him with bright, friendly eyes.

"Where . . . where's the mother?" Pete quavered.

"Right behind the baby!" cried Bob. "Run for it."

There was an angry bawling. The bear cub scooted in one direction and the boys dashed in another, toward the ski slope.

Pete reached the slope first. He jumped, then let himself roll and tumble until he was twenty yards down the incline. Bob and Jupe came slipping and sliding after him. The three crouched on the dry, stony hillside and listened to the mother bear scolding the cub. The cub yelped sharply.

"She's probably giving it a cuff on the ear," guessed Bob.

"We'll be okay," said Jupe. "So long as we don't threaten the cub, she won't bother us."

"I wouldn't dream of threatening her cub," said Pete warmly. "Rule number one: Never get too near a bear cub when the mother's around. I only wish someone had told the cub about it."

"It knows now," Bob assured him.

The three waited for a while. When no more growls or yelps were heard from the meadow above them, they climbed back up. They were in time to see the mother bear and her baby disappear into the woods on the west side of the meadow.

Jupiter Jones took off his knapsack. "They probably won't come back," he said. "However, this is one place where Mr. Smathers would say we were the intruders, and he would be right. The bears were here first and they're still here, so we'd better watch our steps."

"I plan to," said Pete. "In fact, I may just watch my steps taking me back down to the inn!"

"You don't want to find out what Havemeyer's hunting with his tranquilizer gun?" asked Bob.

"Yes, I guess I do," admitted Pete. "Only I don't think I want to meet it face to face!"

From his knapsack, Jupe took three small devices. "We can cover the ground faster if we separate," he said. "But we had better not get out of touch with each other. We don't really know what we're looking for or what we might meet, so I brought along the directional signal and emergency alarm units. I packed them at home because I thought they'd come in handy on a hike, and indeed they will."

Pete sighed. "They're better than nothing," he said. He took one of the devices from Jupiter and turned it over in his hands. "You sure it's working okay?" he asked. "I'd hate to get marooned up here and not be able to call for help."

"I tested all three signals before we left Rocky Beach," said Jupiter. "They're in perfect order. You remember how they work?"

"Like most of your inventions, they work just fine," said Bob.

It was true. Jupiter Jones had a way of putting together salvaged bits of machinery or electronic equipment and turning out devices which served The Three Investigators well while they worked on many of their cases. The directional signal and emergency alarm was smaller than the walkie-talkies which the boys sometimes used, but it was still effective. Each unit broadcast a signal—a beep—which could be picked up by every other unit, and which got louder and faster the nearer one approached it. Each of the units also had a dial to indicate the direction a beep was coming from.

In addition to being a sending and receiving set for electronic beeps, each unit had a special alarm—a red light which could be activated by voice alone. When one of The Three Investigators was in trouble or wanted the others to come to him, he had only to say the word "help" near his set, and the red lights flashed on the other units.

"Now, here's what I suggest we do." Jupiter paused and scanned the woods which rimmed the meadow. "I think it unlikely that we'll find many footprints here in the open," he said. "The grass is too thick. Besides, if there is some strange animal here, it must be sheltered back away from the meadow or we'd have seen it by now. Yet we know it has come out into the open, because Joe Havemeyer told Anna he saw it on the meadow. That means it had to come through the trees to get here. The ground is clear under those trees; there isn't any grass. If we're going to pick up any strange tracks, that's where we'll find them."

"Makes sense," said Bob.

"So why don't I search the woods on the north side of the meadow?" said Jupiter. "I can work my way west from the ski slope. Pete, you could take the woods to the west. You might start at the big white stone and go south. Bob, do you want to go over the ground on the south side? You could start from here and keep going until you meet Pete. Every few minutes we can signal one another on our directional finders, and if something looks threatening or especially interesting, we'll activate the alarms."

"I'll sure do that," promised Pete.

Jupiter put his knapsack on his shoulders, saluted his friends with one hand, and went off to the right. Pete grinned, as if to show he was really not scared, and headed west through the long grass. Bob hesitated a moment, listening to the lonely sound the wind made on the quiet mountain. Then, holding his directional signal in one hand, he trudged to the south.

He looked back once. Jupiter had vanished among the trees on the north side of the meadow. He could see Pete, who had almost reached his section of the woods. Bob activated his directional signal. An answering beep came from Jupiter. Another beep came from Pete, who turned and waved across the meadow.

When he reached the woods on the south side of the field, Bob paused. In the open, under the blue sky, the early morning sun had been bright and warm. But the woods looked very dim and very dense. There was a pungent carpet of pine needles under the trees.

Bob began to walk west, not quite venturing in under the trees. He watched the ground as he went, stopping every few seconds to listen. He heard a jay cry out from some hidden place. A squirrel scampered along a branch.

Then he saw it. It was a faint depression, a place where some large creature had tramped down the earth under the trees and dislodged a few pine needles.

Bob touched the signal on his directional device. After a second, there was an answering beep from the north, and a second from the northwest. He considered shouting for help, to bring Jupe and Pete running to see his find, but there was nothing distinct about the track. He knew it was very likely another bear, or perhaps even a smaller animal. He decided to search farther in, under the trees, to see if he could find a better print.

He went into the dimness under the trees. Here and there he found patches of clear earth, and he hopefully examined these, but there were no more tracks. Twice he found places where fallen pine needles had been pressed down when some animal stepped on them, but the needles were strewn so thickly on the ground that they would not take a clear imprint. There was nothing that could be called a definite track.

Bob went on. The trees grew more closely together. The light grew dimmer, and at last the blue sky was hidden by the interlacing branches. Then, ahead, Bob saw brightness. He went more quickly, and stepped out from under the trees into a small clearing. Almost at his feet was what looked like a huge crack in the earth.

Bob edged forward and looked down into the crevice. It was a split in the ground almost fifty yards long and, in the widest places, about ten feet across. The sides were so sheer that they were almost straight up and down. At the bottom of this peculiar opening in the earth was snow, still unmelted by the summer warmth.

Bob knew what it was. While working at his part-time job at the library in Rocky Beach, he had come across a book of maps of hiking trails in the San Gabriel Mountains and the Sierras. One map of trails in the Mammoth Lakes area showed a similar crevice, caused by an earthquake that had fractured the ground. The temperature at the bottom of the Mammoth fracture, many feet below the surface, was like the temperature in a cave. It was cool even on the hottest day, so the snow that fell during the winter never completely melted.

The beep sounded on Bob's directional signal. It was Jupe, reporting his whereabouts on the north side of the meadow. A second beep came in, and the needle swung westward. Bob activated his own device to answer his friends, wishing that they had brought the walkie-talkies. The discovery of an earthquake fracture within a mile or so of Anna's inn was something Bob would have liked to share immediately.

Bob gazed along the rim of the crevice. The earth was bare, and in spite of the dry season it still held some moisture. When Bob stepped back from the split in the ground, he could see the imprint of his own sneakers. Perfect for tracking!

He began to walk along the edge of the crevice, examining the ground inch by inch.

Behind Bob, and to his left, a branch snapped.

Bob stood still and listened. A second ticked by, and two and three. After that single sound, the quiet was intense. Too intense. No birds called and no squirrels chattered in the trees. Even the wind had died. It was as if all the creatures who made their home on Mount Lofty were sitting motionless, watching and waiting.

Waiting for what?

A muscle in the back of Bob's leg twitched. He shook himself and cleared his throat. "Stop that!" he said, and his voice was loud in the stillness. "Get a grip on yourself. You're letting your imagination run away with you!"

He listened again, and only heard the blood rushing in his ears. Then he heard something else—something horribly close. Behind him, almost at his shoulder, there was the sound of breathing.

Slowly, very slowly so as not to startle whatever it was, Bob began to turn.

There was a warmth on his neck, and then a touch— a soft touch, a mere brushing against his shirt collar.

Bob jumped, twisting in midair, trying to face the being that had come out of the woods.

Afterward, Bob couldn't tell who screamed first, himself or the creature that had crept up on him. He only knew that his ears were ringing, shattered with sound, and that he was looking into a pair of dark, red-rimmed eyes. He had an impression of hugeness and matted hair. Then he was staggering, slipping on the clean earth at the edge of the crevice.

He fell. He fell backward and saw sky, and then the steep, bare walls of the earthquake fracture. His body twisted and snow at the bottom of the pit rushed up at him.

He felt the impact on his hands and knees and heard another scream. Then he blacked out.

10

The Naked Footprint

Bob opened his eyes. He slowly focused on snow and the brown, muddy walls of the crevice. He lay without moving, and listened. There were no more screams. There was no sound of breathing. Instead, from high above him came the trilling of a bird.

Carefully, slowly, he rolled over until he was on his back. His hands hurt and there was a pain in one shoulder, but nothing seemed to be broken. The snow at the bottom of the fracture had helped break his fall, though it had been too packed down to provide a soft landing.

Bob looked up at sunlight and blue sky. He remembered his glimpse of red-rimmed eyes and of matted hair on the creature who had come so close to him. He thought of giants prowling Sky Village, on the lookout for children who might have lingered out after dark.

After several minutes, he stood up, shivering from the chill of the grainy snow. His directional signal lay a few feet away from him. He picked it up, hoping fervently that the fall hadn't broken it. It emitted a shrill, important little "beep" and the needle on the dial swung to the north. Bob smiled. Jupiter Jones was reporting in.

Bob held the signal and looked up to the rim of the crevice. The walls of the earthquake fracture were very steep. He knew he would never be able to climb out without help. He would have to summon Jupe and Pete. But what if the creature still waited above, near the crevice? He might be calling his two friends into danger.

Bob considered this for a moment, then decided to find out if the beast was still up there. He was sure no animal would knowingly leap into a pit. He could safely shout and see if the thing looked down at him.

"Hello!" he cried. "Hello up there! Are you there?"

Nothing moved near the rim of the crevice. After a few minutes, Bob decided that the animal was gone. He held up his directional signal and shouted, "Help!" Then, to be sure that the unit had registered his alarm, he shouted twice more. If Pete and Jupe were within two miles of him, he knew that their units would pick up his signal.

He activated his unit so that it sent out its directional beep to guide his friends to the crevice. Then he sat down on the snow and waited.

It seemed to Bob that he waited hours. But it was only fifteen minutes before Pete looked down into the fracture. Jupiter's round face appeared a moment later.

"Bob, are you all right?" asked Jupiter.

"How the heck did you get down there?" Pete wanted to know.

"I fell," said Bob.

"No kidding!"

"You'd have fallen, too, if you'd seen what I saw," declared Bob.

"What did you see?" asked Jupe.

"Some animal—something big. I don't know what it was. It came up behind me and . . . look, let's go into the details later. Right now, I need to get out of here."

Jupiter measured the depth of the crevice with his eye. "Rope," he decided. "We'll need a rope."

"I'll get it," Pete volunteered. "I saw some yesterday when we were looking for the key. There's a coil of clothesline in one of the kitchen cupboards."

"You can make better time than I can," said Jupiter. "You're the athlete in the group. Get back to the inn as fast as you can and get the rope. I'll stay here with Bob."

Pete nodded. "Watch yourself," he cautioned.

"Don't worry," said Jupiter.

Pete sprinted off through the trees and Jupe crouched at the edge of the crevice. "What did you see?" he asked Bob again.

"Honestly, Jupe, I can't be sure. It happened so fast. I heard something behind me, and something touched me, and I turned around and . . . well, I saw eyes— really strange eyes. It was practically breathing in my face. I yelled, and I think it yelled. Then I fell."

"Another bear?" said Jupe.

"Jupe, I really don't think so."

Jupe stood up and began to walk slowly along the edge of the fracture, peering at the ground.

"Jupe?" Bob called. "You still there?"

"I'm here," Jupe's voice floated down. "I can see your tracks on the ground up here. Whatever came up behind you should have left a track, too. If it was a bear, we'll find the same kind of track we found on the meadow."

"If it wasn't a bear," said Bob, "we may have found what we came looking for."

Jupiter didn't answer right away. Bob waited, then called, "Jupe?"

"I can't believe it!" exclaimed Jupe.

"What is it?" called Bob.

"Bob, are you sure it wasn't a man who came up behind you?" Jupe's voice was squeaky with excitement. "A very big man in his bare feet?"

"I didn't see any feet, and if that was a man I may resign from the human race," said Bob.

"That's amazing," said Jupe. "Someone—some very big person—has been here in bare feet."

Bob thought again of Gabby Richardson and his tales of monsters on the mountain. Hadn't there been one story about a trapper who found the print of a naked foot high up, on the edge of a glacier?

"Jupe?" cried Bob. "Hey, Jupe, be careful, huh?"

Jupe didn't answer, but Bob heard him give a little gasp.

"Jupe?" shouted Bob.

Still there was no answer, but Bob heard a branch break in the woods, and then a shushing, swishing sound from the edge of the crevice.

"Jupe, what are you doing up there?" Bob was shouting, and he felt the back of his neck prickle with fear.

The scraping, sweeping sound above ceased and there was complete silence. Bob called again and again, but Jupe didn't respond. Filled with a dread that was almost panic, Bob tried to find a foothold in the walls of the crevice. There was none. He looked around for something—a fallen branch, anything—that he could use to try to climb out of the pit. There was nothing but the snow and the sheer walls of earth.

Bob finally stopped calling. He stood at the bottom of the pit and waited and listened. And he heard a groan.

"Jupe?"

"Ugh!" It was Jupiter's voice. "Oh, my neck!"

"What happened?" cried Bob. "Where'd you go?"

Jupiter looked over the edge of the fracture. Bob saw that his head was held to one side and that he was rubbing his neck. "I didn't go anywhere," he said. "Somebody came up behind me and hit me."

"Your neck?" asked Bob. "Did you get rabbit punched, like Mr. Jensen?"

"I got rabbit punched like Mr. Jensen," Jupiter confirmed. "Also, while I was unconscious, someone went to the trouble of sweeping the earth all around this crevice with a pine branch. There isn't a single footprint left up here, naked or otherwise!"

11

The Photographer's Notebook

"There's one thing we know for sure," said Bob after Pete had finally arrived with the rope and he had been pulled out of the crevice. "It wasn't a bear that gave you a rabbit punch, Jupe."

"It most certainly was not," agreed Jupiter Jones. "Bears don't break branches off pine trees and use them to sweep the ground. You were startled by something—possibly by a very large barefooted man—and it may have been the same barefooted creature who punched me and then erased his own tracks."

Pete stared at his two friends as if they were losing their minds. "A barefooted man?" he said. "Nobody runs around up here in bare feet."

"Jupe found the print of a naked foot on the edge of the crevice," Bob explained.

"A very large footprint," said Jupe. "I'd say it must have been at least eighteen inches long."

"Eighteen inches? A human footprint eighteen inches long?"

"It looked like a human footprint," said Jupe. "It wasn't a bear—that I know."

Pete coiled the clothesline with hands that were shaking slightly. "Monster Mountain," he said. "The old-timers called this place Monster Mountain. And it looks like there is a monster on it. . . ."

"Monster?" said a sharp voice almost at Pete's elbow.

Pete jumped.

"Sorry. Did I startle you?" It was little Mr. Smathers. He had come silently through the woods and was standing smiling at the boys. "What's all this talk about monsters?" he wanted to know. "And what does a monster's footprint look like? Where is it? I'd like to see it."

"Someone swept it away," explained Jupiter.

"Of course, of course." Mr. Smathers used the tone of one who will listen politely to a tall tale, but who doesn't believe a word of it.

"There *was* a footprint!" insisted Pete. "If Jupe says he found it, he found it."

Mr. Smathers' apparent good humor deserted him, and his face took on a reddish color. "You've been talking to that Richardson fellow who runs the gas station," he accused them. "I've heard some of his wild yarns. He ought to be ashamed, scaring youngsters that way. I've a good mind to have a word with him."

Mr. Smathers suddenly looked determined. "Yes, that's what I'll do," he announced. "I'll have a word with him and tell him to keep his ghost stories to himself."

Smathers started off at a rapid pace, headed for the village, then turned back toward the boys.

"Not that there aren't dangers here for you," he warned. "You're the intruders here, and the wild creatures don't understand you the way they understand me. They might not mean to harm you, but accidents do happen. I intend to tell Mrs. Havemeyer's cousins to keep you closer to the inn."

"I kind of agree with him on that last part," said Pete when Smathers had gone. "I think we ought to stay away from here. A guy could get hurt tangling with monsters."

"Mr. Smathers has just done a very interesting thing," said Jupiter. "He has just told us that he intends to make sure no one believes us if we tell what happened here this morning. He has also warned us to stay away from here or we may get hurt. Now I'm *sure* that some strange creature—human or animal—lives up here, and Mr. Smathers knows about it. But he doesn't want anyone else to know."

"I think you're right," said Bob. "But I think Mr. Smathers is right, too. We ought to get out of here. I got too close to whatever it is."

Jupe nodded, and the boys set out rapidly toward the meadow. They came through the trees and into the open in time to see Mr. Smathers start down the ski slope. By the time they reached the top of the slope, Smathers was at the bottom.

"He moves fast," said Bob.

"It's downhill all the way," Pete pointed out, and he began a slipping, sliding, half-running descent of the slope. Bob and Jupe followed more carefully.

They were nearly at the bottom when they saw Joe Havemeyer start up the slope. Cousin Anna's husband had a knapsack on his back and his tranquilizer gun slung over his shoulder. When the boys approached him, he stood still. There was a scowl on his face.

"What have you boys been doing?" he asked.

"Hiking," said Pete innocently.

Havemeyer pointed to Bob. "Smathers told me one of you fell in that earthquake fracture. It was you, wasn't it?"

"You knew about the fracture?" asked Jupiter Jones.

"It's not a secret. It'll be a big attraction if we can get the hikers here in the summer. But in the meantime, I want you boys to stay out of the high country. Anna and I would feel responsible if you got hurt. There's not only the chance that you'll fall, but the bears . . ."

"Bears?" Jupiter said. He looked steadily at Havemeyer and then at the tranquilizer gun. "Is that why you carry that gun, Mr. Havemeyer?" he asked. "It's a tranquilizer gun, isn't it? Are you planning to capture a bear with it?"

Havemeyer laughed. "Capture a bear? Now, why would I want to do a thing like that? No, I'm not planning to capture any bears and I think it would probably be against the law. I just want to be ready if I meet one, and I don't want to hurt anything." He paused and grinned. "Mr. Smathers would never forgive me if I hurt a bear!"

Havemeyer passed them and toiled on up the slope.

"Mr. Smathers just made a mistake," Bob said.

"Right," said Pete. "We didn't tell him that you fell in the hole, so if he knew it, he must have been there when it happened—or when Jupe got hit."

"He may even have been the one who hit me," said Jupe, "and he is probably the one who swept away the footprint from the edge of the crevice. Our Mr. Smathers may not be as nonviolent as he seems. There is something in the high country—monster or not—that both he and Havemeyer have seen, and they both want to keep it a secret."

The boys reached the backyard of the inn just as Konrad climbed out of the swimming pool excavation. "Hey, Jupe!" he called.

Jupe waved. The Three Investigators went to the hole and looked down to see Hans sitting on the bottom, taking a rest. The forms for the cement were almost finished. "Good hike?" asked Hans.

"Very interesting," said Jupe.

"Hardly a dull moment," Pete added.

"You make Mr. Smathers very nervous," Konrad said. "He does not want you up near that meadow. He tells us we should make you stay down here."

"Do you think you're going to do that?" Pete asked.

Konrad grinned. "I think you will do what you want," he said. "Only you be careful, okay?"

"We'll be careful," Jupiter promised. "Where's Mr. Smathers now?"

"He walked down to the village," said Hans. "Cousin Anna, she took the car and went to Bishop to buy some things. Mr. Jensen went someplace in his car, too."

"Cousin Anna says you should eat some lunch when you come back," Konrad told them. "There are sandwiches in the refrigerator."

"I'm ready," said Pete.

After the boys had wolfed down lunch, Jupiter washed the dishes. Cousin Anna's wedding ring was on the window sill over the sink. Jupe frowned. "That ring's too big for Anna," he said. "She's going to lose it if she doesn't watch out."

Pete, who was drying the glasses, only nodded absently. His attention had been caught by something on the living room floor, just beyond the kitchen doorway. He put the dish towel on the drainboard and went to the living room.

"Somebody's wallet," he said, and stooped to pick it up.

It was an old wallet, worn soft and with one seam ripped. When Pete picked it up a cascade of cards and papers slipped out onto the floor.

"Oh, blast!" Pete crouched to gather up the things.

"Whose is it?" Bob called.

Pete found a driver's license among the business

cards and restaurant receipts which littered the floor. "It's Mr. Jensen's," he said. "Boy, he's out with his car now. I hope he doesn't get stopped by the police for running a red light or anything. They'll really nail him if he's driving without his license."

"Just a minute." Jupiter had come to the doorway, and he was staring down at a snapshot which lay on the floor. "That's Cousin Anna," he said.

"Huh?" said Bob. "What?"

"A picture of Cousin Anna." Jupe bent and picked it up.

It was a picture of Anna Havemeyer and her husband. They had been snapped coming out of a coffee shop in some city or town, and evidently were not aware of the camera. Anna wore a light-colored shirt-waist dress and had a sweater over her shoulders. Her head was half-turned so that she looked back at Joe Havemeyer. His mouth was open and his expression was determined. He seemed to be saying something important to his wife.

"What's Jensen doing with a picture of Anna in his wallet?" asked Jupiter. He handed the snapshot to Bob.

Pete finished gathering up Mr. Jensen's belongings, then took the snapshot from Bob and studied it. "It sure wasn't taken here in Sky Village," he said. He turned the picture over and looked at the back. "There's a date on it—it was taken last week, in Lake Tahoe."

The Three Investigators looked blankly at one another.

"Is Jensen an old friend of Anna's?" Bob wondered. "Or of Havemeyer's? Could he have been at their wedding?"

"No!" said Jupe firmly. "The first night we were here they had a party for Anna's wedding, and Jensen and Smathers were the outsiders. Don't you remember? Havemeyer said they'd have to include the paying guests, but they wouldn't let Mr. Jensen and Mr. Smathers spoil things."

Pete slipped the snapshot into the wallet. "Mr. Jensen may be only a paying guest, but he *does* have a picture of the Havemeyers taken in Tahoe. That's quite a coincidence!"

Jupiter took the wallet from Pete. "I believe we should simply put this on Mr. Jensen's bureau and not say anything about it," he said virtuously. "And while we're in his room, we might keep our eyes open for anything of interest. Since we have been asked by Hans and Konrad to help protect Cousin Anna, it is our duty to look for threats from all directions. . . ."

"I get your meaning," said Pete. "Let's move on it, huh, before somebody gets back!"

Jensen's room was on the north side of the house, next to the big double room occupied by Hans and Konrad.

"Hope it's not locked," said Bob.

"Nothing in this place ever gets locked," said Pete. He turned the knob and Mr. Jensen's door swung open.

The room was neat and clean, like everything else in the inn. A poplin windbreaker had been thrown over the back of a chair and a comb tossed down on the bureau. Other than that, there were no signs that anyone occupied the place.

Jupe opened the closet door and found a good supply of sport shirts, some creased from wear and others fresh and clean. A pair of black oxfords were on the floor, and next to them was Jensen's suitcase.

Jupe hefted the suitcase. "Not all unpacked," he said. He carried the case to the bed, where he put it down and opened it.

There were socks in the suitcase, and clean underwear, several rolls of film, and a few packages of flash bulbs. There was also a book. Pete whistled with delight when Jupe picked it up.

"*Photography for Beginners*," he read.

Jupe opened the book at random. "Not what one would expect to find in the luggage of a successful commercial photographer," he said. "If Jensen is selling his work to magazines, he should be far too expert to need this sort of handbook. It's very elementary." He closed the book. "Whatever he is, Mr. Jensen is not a photographer."

Bob began to lift socks and underwear out of the suitcase. "Let's see what else there is," he said.

He discovered nothing else except a little notebook which was greatly worn and dog-eared, and which was crammed with names, addresses, and telephone numbers. Bob went through the book quickly. Most of the addresses were for businesses or individuals in Lake Tahoe. There was no entry for Cousin Anna until the very end of the book. There, on a page that was otherwise blank, was a series of notations that caused Bob's eyes to widen with astonishment.

"You found something?" asked Jupe.

"There's a page here all about Cousin Anna," said Bob. "Look, there's a number at the top—PWU 615, California. Then Anna's name—Miss Anna Schmid—and her address, Slalom Inn, Sky Village, California."

"PWU 615?" said Pete. "Sounds like the license number of a car."

"Anything else?" asked Jupe.

Bob handed the notebook to Jupe without another word.

"Fascinating," said Jupe. "A notation that Anna owns the Slalom Inn and also the ski tow, and that she has the reputation in Sky Village of paying cash for everything. And written at the bottom of the page, the words, 'A perfect pigeon!'"

"Pigeon?" said Pete. "That's con-man talk, isn't it?"

"Yes," answered Jupe. He closed the notebook and put it back into the suitcase. "It's a term used by swindlers. A pigeon is a sucker, a victim, an easy mark."

"So Jensen is a confidence man, and Anna is his victim."

"At least Jensen is not a photographer," said Jupe. "But if he's a swindler, what is he up to? He hasn't done a thing here except . . ."

"Except get rabbit punched by a bear, or a monster, or whatever," Pete finished. "He hasn't even been especially friendly with Anna."

They heard a car on the road outside. Jupe hurried

across the hall to the room occupied by Mr. Smathers. He looked out the window.

"It's Cousin Anna returning from Bishop," he reported, "and the license number of her car *is* PWU 615."

Bob hastily closed the suitcase and stowed it back in the closet. Pete smoothed the bed where it had rested.

"Do we warn her she's got a con man registered here?" asked Pete as the boys left the room.

Jupe shook his head. "I don't think we should do that without real proof. We only know that Jensen has a snapshot of Anna and Havemeyer taken in Tahoe the week they were married, and that he's particularly interested in Anna's finances. Bob, you're going to talk to your father tonight to get the report on Havemeyer. Let's give him Jensen's address from his driver's license—I noticed that he lives in Tahoe Valley—and see if your father's contact in Reno can find out anything about Jensen. And until we know more, we had better keep an eye on our supposed photographer whenever he's around Cousin Anna. If he tries to interest her in some moneymaking scheme, we'd better be ready!"

12

Another Searcher

The Three Investigators came down the stairs to find Anna in the living room, adding several new magazines to a stack on an end table. She started slightly when she heard them. "Oh," she said. "I did not know anyone was here."

"We were searching again," Jupe explained with a straight face. "We thought we might have overlooked something yesterday when we tried to find the key to your safe deposit box."

"Oh, yes. The key." Anna's forehead creased in a worried frown. "You did not find it today?"

"No," said Bob. "Mrs. Havemeyer, has it occurred to you that someone might have taken it? The doors here are never locked. Anyone could have walked in here and picked it up."

"Not when I have hidden it so well," said Anna.

"And no one will wish to take the key if he knows what it is for. Only Anna Schmid can use that key. The people at the bank know only Anna Schmid. Anyone who steals the key gains nothing. But he causes trouble for me. That is why I hid the key when I left for Lake Tahoe."

"There goes the burglar theory," said Pete.

"The key must be here somewhere," said Anna. "If only I could remember where."

Outside, gravel crunched as a car came up the drive. Then Jensen came in. He had his camera case in one hand. He nodded to Anna and the boys and went upstairs.

"Interesting work Mr. Jensen does," said Jupiter. "It must take a lot of patience to photograph animals. Does he come here often?"

"It is the first time," said Anna. "He came only five days ago. He did not write first, so he did not have a reservation, but I had the room and I could take him."

"Mr. Smathers is an interesting person, too," said Jupe. "I imagine he spends a great deal of time in the mountains, communing with nature."

"You mean talking with the animals? I wonder, do they listen? But for him it is the first time, too. He says he wants to be here because we have so dry a season. He thinks he can help his wild friends to keep out of trouble." Cousin Anna laughed. "Such an idea. Such a strange little man. Only I wish he would eat like everyone else and I would not have to make special things for him."

Cousin Anna went out to the kitchen and the boys

heard her opening cupboards and banging pots. They drifted out the front door of the inn and down the road past the pine grove to the gasoline station, where Gabby Richardson sat drowsing in the afternoon sun. Richardson opened his eyes as the boys approached.

"Have a good hike?" he wanted to know.

"You've been talking to Mr. Smathers," said Pete.

"I wouldn't say that," Richardson told them. "He's been talking to me. Seems to think I'm corrupting the youth of America by telling them monster tales." Richardson's sleepy eyes narrowed, and suddenly he was most alert, most curious. "What *did* you see on the mountain this morning?"

"We're not sure, Mr. Richardson," said Bob. "Something big. Some animal, I think."

Gabby Richardson looked keenly disappointed. "Bears, most likely—or a bear. You the one who fell into the earthquake fracture?"

Bob admitted that he was.

"Thought so," said Richardson. "That sort of thing doesn't do your clothes a bit of good. Not hurt, I see."

"No," Bob told him. "Just shaken up a little."

"Got to watch your step in that wild country," said Richardson. "You look like sensible lads. I'm sure you didn't bother that bear any. No need for Anna Schmid to get so riled up about it. Or I guess I should say Anna Havemeyer."

"She's upset?" said Pete. "We just saw her and she didn't seem upset."

"Well, maybe she got over it by now. She stopped here for gas on her way back from Bishop, and that oddball Smathers had just been here, so I asked her if she'd talked to you after your hike. You may have noticed, I like to keep track of what goes on around here."

"We've noticed." Pete laughed.

"So she said her husband didn't want you up on the meadow because of the bears. Marriage sure hasn't improved that woman. She's gotten nervous as a city dude about those critters. I remember the day she'd charge out yelling and waving a skillet at them if they so much as sniffed at her trash."

Bob looked startled. "Is that really a good idea?" he asked. "I mean, they *are* wild and . . ."

"So long as you don't get too close to them, and you don't actually hit them, it works sometimes."

Bob looked at his watch. "It's after four," he said to Jupe. "I'm sure my dad will be home by now. I'll put in the call to him."

"Phone not working at the inn?" asked Gabby Richardson.

"It isn't that," Bob said quickly. "We just happened to be down this way, so I thought . . ."

"Sure, sure," said Richardson. "Well, don't let me stop you. You go ahead and make your telephone call. Me, I'm going over to the pizza house and have a bite. I know when to mind my own business."

The man got up and ambled slowly out of the station and up the street.

"The day that guy minds his own business, I'll eat my tennis shoes without salt," said Pete in a low voice.

Bob laughed and stepped into the telephone booth.

After talking to his father for five minutes, he reported, "Joe Havemeyer isn't listed in the Reno telephone book. The credit bureau in Reno hasn't come through with a report on him yet, but Dad's friend expects it tomorrow. Dad will call his friend tonight and ask him to check on Jensen, too, but he says we are not to go off half-cocked and make any trouble for anybody, because if we embarrass Hans and Konrad or their cousin for no good reason he will skin us alive. We are to do nothing until we hear from him—except move out of the inn."

"Oh?" said Jupiter Jones.

"He's afraid we're imposing on Cousin Anna, and I guess we are. There's no special reason she should be feeding us, is there? We're not her relations."

"Just when things were really getting interesting," said Pete.

"We don't need to move far," Jupe pointed out. "Our tent is already pitched near the house."

The Three Investigators returned to the inn, where they told Cousin Anna and her husband that they intended to follow their original plan and camp out. There were some protests from Joe Havemeyer, and warnings about prowling bears, but the boys promised to shout for help if they saw or heard anything menacing. Well before sunset they had moved their sleeping bags out to the tent and had set up camp in earnest.

After a dinner of frankfurters and beans cooked over an open fire, the boys sat cross-legged inside the tent. Bob took a notebook and a ball-point pen out of his pocket and began to jot down the investigators' findings on their current case.

"So far," he said, "we have a nature photographer who isn't a photographer at all, and who is very interested in Cousin Anna and her money.

"He also has a photograph of Anna and her husband, taken before he came to the inn. Yet Anna told us this is his first time here, and she doesn't really know him."

"And he got swatted by a bear, or a person, or a monster," added Pete. "If he isn't a photographer, I wonder why he bothered to take that picture of the bear at the trash cans."

"He no doubt felt that he should behave like a photographer, since that's what he claims to be," decided Jupiter. "So much for Mr. Jensen. Then we have Anna's new husband. What do we know about him?"

"He says he has a good income," said Bob. "Owns a tranquilizer gun and goes with it to the high meadow every day. Is building a swimming pool which may not be a swimming pool at all."

Bob looked at Jupe. "Can you think of anything else? That's not much. Hans and Konrad are nervous about him, but he may be completely on the level."

"He may be," agreed Jupe.

"Then there's Mr. Smathers," said Pete. "He's really some kind of a nut."

"And not as harmless as he looks," said Jupe. "I'm sure it was Smathers who knocked me out this morning and erased the footprint from the edge of the crevice."

"Which brings us to the big question mark," Pete

said. "Is there or is there not a monster on Monster Mountain?"

"I saw something," said Bob. "I know I saw something, and I'm pretty darn sure it wasn't a bear. And Jupe saw that footprint."

Jupiter unzipped his sleeping bag and slipped his shoes off. "If there *is* a monster and Joe Havemeyer catches it, things will be very lively around here," he predicted. "Let's remember that our clients are Hans and Konrad and our concern is to protect their cousin. Tomorrow, when we get the credit report on Havemeyer and some more information about Jensen, we can talk with Hans and Konrad. They can decide what they want to do, if anything."

Bob and Pete dropped off quickly that night, but Jupiter Jones was too restless to sleep. He lay awake and listened to the wind and to the small rustlings and scurryings made by wild creatures in the darkness. He thought of the crevice in the earth, and of that incredible naked footprint. He thought of Gabby Richardson and his story of strange beings on the mountain. And he thought of another of Gabby's tales—his description of Anna charging at a bear, swinging a skillet. Jupe resolved that he would ask Anna in the morning if she had really done such a rash thing.

It was nearly midnight when Jupe rolled over on his stomach and opened the flap of the tent. The Slalom Inn was dark and quiet. A small shadow flitted overhead, lighted on the chimney of the inn, and stayed there for several minutes. Jupe heard a faint hoot. It was an owl.

Jupe blinked. Had he imagined it, or had there been a flicker of light somewhere on the lower floor of the inn? He watched intently. It came again, a moving beam in the living room, beyond the office.

Jupe poked Pete. "Wake up!" he whispered.

"Wha . . . what's the matter?" Pete sat up. "More bears?"

"Hey, quiet!" said Bob sleepily.

"Someone's up at the inn," said Jupe. "With a flashlight. Look, someone's gone into Anna's office."

Pete and Bob rolled out of their sleeping bags and fumbled in the dark for their shoes. "Here we go again!" said Pete. "*Everybody's* interested in Cousin Anna—or her money or her office."

The Three Investigators crawled out of their tent and stole across the yard to the office window. It was open, and the boys could see the man who sat in the desk chair, with his back to them. Jensen! He was quietly going through one of Anna's ledgers, holding his flashlight in one hand. The door between the office and the living room was now closed.

Jensen finished his examination of one ledger and put it aside on the bookcase. He was just reaching for a second book when he stiffened and cocked an ear toward the door. A second later he dived into the knee-hole under the desk and snapped off his light.

The Three Investigators ducked down below the window frame. The overhead light in the office clicked on, and the boys heard Joe Havemeyer's voice.

"You see?" said Havemeyer. "There's no one here."

"I heard someone," said Anna. "I know I heard

someone on the stairs, and then the door closed. I think I left the door open. I think . . . I cannot be sure."

"You're imagining things, letting your nerves get the best of you. There's nothing to worry about. You're doing beautifully with those two clods from Rocky Beach. Don't let them get to you. They won't stay forever."

"More than a week," said Cousin Anna. "They will be here for more than a week."

"I'm keeping them busy, aren't I? Now take it easy. We're set, you know, and nothing will go wrong."

"Nothing had better," said Cousin Anna. There was an edge to her voice that convinced Jupe that she *had* driven off marauding bears with a skillet.

The office light snapped off and the door closed. The boys stayed where they were, not moving. After a few minutes they saw the flashlight beam again. Jensen was up from behind the desk. He crossed to the office door, turned off his light, and very quietly left the office.

"I'll be darned," whispered Pete.

Jupe put a warning finger to his lips. The three crept away from the inn and back to their tent.

"Did I hear what I thought I heard?" said Pete, when they were safely inside the tent.

"Very, very peculiar," said Jupiter Jones. "I am not especially surprised that Jensen came down in the middle of the night to search through Anna's records. We know he's interested in her money."

"Right," said Bob. "Only why should Anna be nervous about Hans and Konrad? Her own favorite cousins."

"It doesn't make sense." Jupe rubbed his forehead. "Nothing makes sense. I've never been so bewildered in my life."

13

Cousin Anna's Homework

Jupiter awoke to chill morning sunlight and birdsong. Pete and Bob were still asleep, so he put on his shoes and got out of the tent without making a sound. He crossed the yard to the back door of the inn, pondering in a groggy, half-awake way on Joe Havemeyer's words of the night before.

Hans and Konrad were making Anna nervous.

Jupe paused at the foot of the back steps. He heard water running in the sink beyond the open window. Anna must be up, he decided. He could picture her in the kitchen, her thin, capable hands moving surely. They were not the hands of a fearful woman. Anna did things as easily and quickly as Aunt Mathilda. In fact, thought Jupiter, Anna was much like Aunt Mathilda. She even took off her wedding ring before she did dishes, as Aunt Mathilda did when she had been on one of her sporadic diets and her ring was too big for her.

Jupe was about to go into the inn and wish Anna a good morning when the water stopped running.

"Coffee not ready yet?" It was Havemeyer's voice.

"A few minutes. Don't be so impatient," said Anna.

"Don't you be so jumpy," warned Havemeyer. "Look, I'll get Hans and Konrad started working this morning, so they won't be under your feet. You invite those kids out there to breakfast, and then pack a lunch for them and send them off on a hike someplace. Anyplace but the high meadow. Make sure they don't head that way."

"You are now a social director?" asked Anna.

"I don't want them in the way," said Havemeyer. "I'm going up the slope for one last try, but I'm not hopeful. If we're stymied, we'll have to bluff it at the bank and you'd better be good. So do your homework."

"I do not want to do it," protested Anna.

"You'll do it." Havemeyer's voice was rough. "You've done harder things, and for less money. You got some stuff for sandwiches for the kids?"

"I have ham." Anna's tone was sulky.

"That'll do."

Jupiter Jones backed away from the porch, then cleared his throat loudly and stomped up the steps.

"Good morning," called Cousin Anna.

Jupiter greeted her brightly and put up only token resistance when she invited him to breakfast. He went upstairs to wash. When he came down again, Bob and

Pete had appeared, still tousled from sleep. Jensen and Smathers sat at the table waiting for their breakfast.

The meal was quiet. Each person seemed busy with private thoughts. Cousin Anna was clearing away cups and saucers afterward when she seemed struck by a happy idea.

"You had a good hike yesterday," she said to the boys. "You should go again today. It is your holiday, and you should have a nice time. I will make you some sandwiches and you can go. There is a good trail from the campground to the fire tower, and I think you should go that way."

"The fire tower!" said Bob. "Oh, that abandoned one we saw the other day. That must be three or four miles from here."

Anna nodded. "And high up. From the tower you can see all the valley. Sometimes, when I am not too busy, I go there to be alone and think."

"Sounds great!" said Jupiter quickly.

Pete opened his mouth to say something, but Jupe kicked him under the table.

Anna carried the dishes to the kitchen and quickly put together a picnic lunch. "You can carry it in your knapsack," she suggested.

The boys thanked her, and Jupe got his knapsack from the tent and stowed the food in the pack.

"Be careful," warned Havemeyer. "We'll expect you back sometime this afternoon. Okay?"

Havemeyer, Konrad, and Hans were setting to work on the swimming pool when the boys started down the road to the campground. As soon as they were around the first bend, Pete stopped. "Am I too suspicious, or is there some special reason we're being shipped off on a hike today?" he asked. "Why did you kick me at breakfast?"

"I overheard Anna and Havemeyer talking this morning," said Jupe. "Havemeyer wants us out of the way so he can go to the high meadow and Anna can do her homework."

"Homework?" echoed Bob.

"Don't ask me what it is," Jupe told them. "It has something to do with the bank. Havemeyer is going up the slope for one last try at something, and if he doesn't succeed this morning he and Anna intend to bluff at the bank. I think it has to do with that safe deposit key Anna wants so desperately to find."

"Shouldn't one of us stay at the inn and find out what she's doing?" asked Pete.

"I don't see how we can," Jupiter said. "She and Havemeyer are determined that she won't be interrupted. They are also determined that we will not be in the high meadow today. We have been very much concerned with protecting Anna, but I begin to wonder whether she needs protection. Whatever Havemeyer is doing, she is his partner, and they're both being extremely secretive. It's ironic that she suggested a hike to that old fire tower. I can't be sure, but I should think you could see not only the valley from that tower, but a lot of the high country. Let's hurry, and we may be in time."

"In time for what?" Bob wanted to know.

"In time to see Joe Havemeyer climb the ski slope,"

said Jupe. "I've got my binoculars in the bottom of the knapsack. Havemeyer goes to the meadow every day with his tranquilizer gun and a knapsack. What does he do there?"

"He's on a monster hunt," said Pete.

"No, there's something else," Jupe said. "Those trips have something to do with the bank, and hence with the missing key. I want to see what Havemeyer does up there."

"Okay," said Bob quickly. "Let's move."

They hurried down the road, across the campground, and then up the trail toward the old fire tower. Pete kept the lead, with Bob close behind him. Jupiter puffed along in the rear. Beyond the campground the trail to the tower climbed sharply, and the boys found themselves bent almost double, leaning into the hillside as they hiked upward.

It was after ten by Pete's watch when they reached the tower.

"I hope we're not too late," gasped Jupiter. Without even stopping to catch his breath, he began to climb the wooden ladder to the top of the tower. Pete and Bob followed.

"Hot diggity!" said Pete. "We can see the inn from here, and the ski slope and the meadow."

Jupe rummaged in his knapsack and took out the binoculars. He put them to his eyes and focused them. "Joe Havemeyer's halfway up the ski slope," he reported.

Jupiter kept the glasses trained on Havemeyer as the man climbed. He reached the meadow after ten minutes and marched straight toward the pine trees on the far side of the open area. In a few minutes, he disappeared into the trees.

Jupe lowered the binoculars. "The western side was yours, Pete. Did you get very far into the trees when we were looking for tracks yesterday?" he asked.

"Not really," Pete answered. "A few yards, maybe. I kept in sight of the meadow."

Havemeyer went in among those trees. Does he go there every day? What could be there?"

"You said his trips have something to do with the bank?" asked Bob. "What could be there that has anything to do with a bank?"

"Trees," said Pete. "More trees. Still more trees. Rocks, squirrels, jays, chipmunks, and . . ."

"Wait a second!" said Jupe suddenly. "The cabin!"

"What cabin?" asked Pete.

"The hermit's cabin. Remember, Gabby Richardson said that the hermit who lived on Monster Mountain built a cabin on the high meadow. We didn't see any building when we were up there. It must be hidden in the trees. That could be where Havemeyer goes!"

"And what does the hermit's cabin have to do with the bank?" asked Bob.

"I don't know," Jupe admitted sadly.

The boys unwrapped the sandwiches Anna had made for them and sat cross-legged in the tower to eat. From time to time Jupiter looked through the binoculars at the meadow and the ski slope. After almost an hour, Havemeyer emerged from the stand of trees to

the west of the meadow and started toward the ski slope.

"He's coming down," said Jupiter. "Now it's our turn to go up there. Look, let's go back to the inn and announce we're going to spend the afternoon at the campground, then cook our dinner there. We'll leave right away with our food and equipment. No one will expect to see us for hours, and we can sneak up to the meadow through the trees on the north side of the ski slope. We've got to find what it is that brings Havemeyer there every day."

"Oh, my aching legs," groaned Pete. He crumpled his sandwich wrapper and put it into Jupe's knapsack. "Let's get started," he said.

The return to the campground was quicker than the trek out to the fire tower. The downhill grade was so steep that the boys had to brace themselves to keep from running.

There was a car parked at the campground when the boys reached it. A short, balding man was looking with dismay at the almost dry creek, while a stout woman unpacked dishes from a picnic basket.

"Pretty sad, isn't it?" said the man, when he saw the boys. "I wanted to get in some fishing."

"It's been a dry season," Bob told him. "The water's low everywhere."

"Harold, let's not stay," said the woman quickly. "Let's go to Bishop and stay in a motel."

"I am *not* spending money on motels when I've got so much tied up in camping gear," said the man. "Anyway, it's cool here." He pointed to the tower. "Does the trail take you up there?" he asked Bob.

"Yes. It's a pretty stiff hike."

The man chortled. "I could use it," he told the boys. "I've let myself get out of condition."

The boys walked on, making good time without actually running, and in fifteen minutes were back at the inn. When they went into the living room, Joe Havemeyer was standing near the fireplace with a piece of paper in his hand.

"Looks fine," he said to Anna, who sat on the sofa.

Anna nodded. Joe glanced at the boys, crumpled the paper, and tossed it into the fireplace. He took a matchbook from the mantle and set fire to the paper, then went up the stairs.

"Good hike?" Anna asked the boys.

"Wonderful!" said Jupe.

"I thought you would like it." Anna got up and went out to the kitchen.

Pete darted to the fireplace and stamped at the slowly burning paper. The flame puffed and died. Pete gingerly picked the remains of the paper out of the fireplace.

There were only a few inches left uncharred, but those few inches were enough.

"What did Havemeyer think looked fine?" Bob asked.

Pete hesitated, then went out onto the front porch. Bob and Jupe followed, and Jupe closed the door behind them.

"Cousin Anna's signature," said Pete. He handed the paper to Jupe. "She's been writing her name over and over."

The Three Investigators were silent for a second. Then Jupe jumped, as if someone had hit him. "She won't speak German with her cousins!" he said suddenly. "She won't speak German, and her wedding ring is too big."

"What do you mean?" asked Bob.

Jupe didn't answer, but he started down the steps. "I'm going to talk to Hans and Konrad right away," he said tensely. "Then we've got to get up to the meadow fast! All of a sudden, everything makes sense to me. If my deductions are correct, something horrible is going on!"

14

The Burning Mountain

"But why, Jupe?" asked Hans. "Why must we stay close to the inn?" He climbed up the ladder out of the swimming pool excavation, leaving Konrad below.

"I'd rather not explain right now," said Jupe. "It would be terribly embarrassing for you—for all of us—if I were wrong. Trust me, please. Just stay here in case I need you."

"Sure, we trust you, Jupe," said Hans. "Okay. Have a good time at the campground," he added uncertainly.

Jupe rejoined Bob and Pete, who had just informed Cousin Anna that they planned to be away for the rest of the day. Quickly the boys gathered what they needed for dinner from their campsite in the pine grove. As they worked, Jensen drove up and Smathers appeared from the trees across the road. Both men climbed onto the front porch of the inn and plopped onto chairs.

Jupe grunted at the sight of them. "I hope they stay right where they are," he said. "I don't know yet how they fit into this."

"Into what, Jupe?" demanded Pete. "What's going on?"

"Later, later," said Jupe impatiently.

The boys were just leaving when Joe Havemeyer walked out onto the front porch.

"Hey, where are you boys going in such a hurry?" he called. His voice was jovial but he looked at them suspiciously.

"Blast!" muttered Jupe. He assumed his best dumb-kid expression and strolled deliberately over to the porch. "We're going down to the campground for a cookout," he said blandly.

"You kids sure have a lot of excess energy," commented Havemeyer. "We ought to keep you right here at the inn and put you to work . . . work . . ."

Havemeyer stopped talking, and his face took on a yellowish tinge. Jupe blinked. Then he realized that it was not Havemeyer who had gone yellow; it was the light which had changed. He looked up to see a thick, billowing cloud of smoke which hid the sun.

"There!" Pete pointed. North of the inn, on the pine-clad slopes beyond the campground, the smoke was thicker and darker. All at once they could see flame. A flake of ash floated down and settled on Havemeyer's hair. Jensen and Smathers left the porch for a better view.

"It's blowing this way," said Havemeyer. It was almost a whisper. The man seemed paralyzed, gripping the porch railing.

There was the roar of a car on the road. The car that had been parked in the campground when the boys came down the mountain was skidding and bumping up toward the inn. Pete raced out, wildly waving his arms, and the car screeched to a stop.

"How bad is it?" Pete shouted to the man.

"Going like crazy!" yelled the man. "You'd better get out of here. Woods are like tinder. Dropped a cigarette and the wind caught a spark and the next thing I knew the whole hillside was burning."

Hans ran out from behind the inn. "Anna!" he shouted. "Anna! Konrad! Come quick. The mountain is on fire!"

The woman in the car cried, "Harold, let's go!" The man stepped on the gas and started so suddenly that his wheels spun on the dusty road.

"Hans! Konrad!" Joe Havemeyer was moving now. He ran down the front steps of the inn and seized a garden hose that lay coiled near the porch. "The ladder!" he shouted to Hans. "Get the ladder. We've got to wet down the roof."

A deer broke from cover across the road and ran blindly up the drive, past the startled humans, toward the ski slope.

"Dear heaven!" Mr. Smathers was so upset that his voice was almost a croak. "Those dreadful people. Criminals! Murderers!" The wildly excited little man scampered after the deer.

"Where are you going?" Mr. Jensen grabbed at Smathers' arm.

A frightened squirrel dashed past Jensen and Smathers and up the ski slope.

"Let me go!" shouted Smathers. "Don't you see? The animals are heading for the high country."

"But the fire's coming this way," warned Jensen. "You'll be trapped up there."

Smathers pulled away from the younger man. "I have to go," he said, and he sprinted toward the slope.

Cousin Anna ran from the house. "Joe!" she cried. "Joe, we have to get out."

"No!" Havemeyer had the water turned on. He backed away from the faucet and aimed the hose toward the roof. "We have to save this place. I know we can save it if we stay with it."

Konrad came up and took Anna's arm. "We will take our cousin and we will get out," he told Havemeyer. "Anna, you come with us, huh?"

Anna turned and looked at the fire. It seemed quite close now, less than a mile from the inn. The wind was hot, and ash speckled the ground.

"You come with us," said Konrad again.

Anna nodded.

"Jupe," said Konrad. "Pete. Bob. Get in the truck."

"Wait a minute!" said Jupiter Jones.

"We cannot wait." Konrad started to lead Anna to the parking area. "Get in the truck!"

"But we have to find Anna," said Jupe.

"What?" Konrad stared at Jupe, then at the woman next to him. She froze in an attitude that had something fiercely defensive about it. It seemed to Jupe that she went pale, but he could not be sure in the murky light.

"Where is Anna?" he demanded.

Havemeyer let the hose drop. "You're crazy!" he said.

Jupe ignored him. "You are Mrs. Havemeyer," he said to the woman called Anna. "Where is Anna Schmid? Tell me. Quickly!"

"Where is Anna Schmid?" Jensen looked like a man who had been struck and stunned. "You are not Anna Schmid?" he said to the woman.

She straightened and seemed to get some grip on herself. "I was Anna Schmid," she said. "Now I am Anna Havemeyer. You know that." She looked Jensen squarely in the face. "I was Anna Schmid, and I will go with my cousins."

"No!" Jupe took two quick steps toward her.

She broke then, and started to run toward her car.

"Hey!" Jensen ran, too, reaching for her shoulder. "One second there."

Anna dodged and stumbled as Jensen's hand caught at her, and she fell. The fair hair with its circle of braids came off like some bizarre hat and rolled for a foot or two before collapsing into a limp heap. Instantly Anna was up again and running. The boys saw that under the wig she had short, bleached hair.

"You are not Anna!" cried Hans.

Konrad caught the woman as she tugged at the door of her car. "Where is my cousin?" he said. He sounded as if he might strike her. "Where is Anna?"

The woman cringed back against the car.

"There's a cabin up near the meadow, isn't there?" said Jupe. "Is she there?"

The woman nodded.

Konrad released her, and a second later he and Hans and The Three Investigators were racing up the slope toward the high country.

15

The Monster

Smoke was thick on the upper meadow when the boys reached it. Jupiter felt that his lungs would burst. He dropped to his knees in the long grass and turned his face away from the hot wind that swept across the mountainside. Ahead of him and to the right, a cougar stalked from the trees, stood for a second as if tasting the scorched air, then ran to the west, to the barren cliffs beyond the trees.

Konrad tugged at Jupe's elbow. "Get up. Quick. Show us where is Anna."

Jupiter stumbled up. Pete was already running across the meadow, making straight for the woods on the far side. Bob ran after, trying valiantly to keep up with Pete. Running with the two boys were animals. Jupe saw that the entire meadow was alive with large and small creatures, all fleeing wildly from the threat of the fire.

"Hurry!" urged Konrad. Hans was ahead of them, following Pete and Bob.

Jupe nodded and forced his trembling legs to carry him across the meadow.

It seemed to Jupe that his legs were made of lead, that he was struggling as if trying to run through deep water. He saw Pete and Bob ahead of him, waiting at the edge of the trees. He stumbled and Konrad grabbed his arm.

"Where?" demanded Konrad.

Jupe pointed to a place where an outcropping of white stone thrust through the grass. "I saw Havemeyer go that way."

A faint scream came to them then, a high, wordless wail of terror, and they heard a distant pounding, as if someone were hammering at a door with clenched fists.

"Anna!" cried Konrad.

A skunk darted across Pete's feet and disappeared among the trees.

The scream came again, louder.

"We are here, Anna!" shouted Hans.

The Three Investigators and the Bavarian brothers charged in through the trees in the direction of the screams and pounding. Pete coughed harshly, and Jupe felt that he was strangling in the dim, smoky air.

"Anna?" shouted Hans. "Where are you, Anna?"

"I am here! Who is it? Let me out!"

The Bavarian brothers raced toward the cry, passing Pete and Bob. They crashed through the woods, breaking branches, flailing with their arms. The boys stumbled after them. Suddenly, in a little gully, there was a cabin.

It was a rude affair of planks covered with tar paper, barely six feet square, with a tiny window high up near the roof. In several places the tar paper had peeled away, but on the crude door was a shiny hasp and a bright, new padlock. When the boys tumbled down the incline into the gully, Hans was heaving at the door with his shoulder.

The door didn't give an inch.

"That is more solid than it looks," said Konrad. "Don't worry, Cousin Anna," he called. "We will get a rock and break the lock."

"There's a fire." The woman's voice inside the cabin was rough with fear. "I smell a fire. Where is it?"

"Below, near the camping place." Konrad had found a stone and was weighing it in his hands. "We still have time. We will get you out."

The woman was silent for a second, then said, "Who is there? Is it . . . is it Hans? Konrad?"

Konrad grinned and broke into a spatter of German, then began to pound at the padlock with the rock.

The wind gusted and blew the smoke thickly around them.

"Hurry!" said Hans.

Konrad nodded, and he raised the rock to give the padlock a mighty blow. And then a scream sounded behind him.

Hans, Konrad, and The Three Investigators whirled around. Above them, glaring down into the gully and beating at the stinging, acrid air, stood a gigantic humanoid figure. Jupe saw eyes glinting red, and he glimpsed teeth when the hairy creature threw back its head and howled with sheer animal terror.

"The monster!" Bob gulped and turned white.

"What is that?" cried the woman in the cabin. "What do I hear?"

"Shhh!" cautioned Jupe.

"Be quiet, Anna," whispered Hans.

But the creature had heard. Anna's cry had reached it through the panic. It lowered its huge head and brushed at the tangle of matted hair that hung almost to its eyes, and it stared through the smoke at Konrad.

Konrad stood frozen with his back to the door, the rock in his hand.

There was a low snarl from the being which had come upon them. The big head lunged forward, and then the beast was rushing at Konrad.

"Watch it!" Pete jumped to one side. The creature charged past, making straight for Konrad as if he had somehow caused the trouble and filled the air with smoke.

Konrad shouted and dived away from the door. The enormous creature crashed on, carried forward by the momentum of its charge. It struck the door, which collapsed inward with a terrible splintering sound. The great beast fell into the cabin on top of it.

And Anna screamed. She screamed as Jupe had never heard a person scream—keen, throat-tearing shrieks of pure terror. And mingled with Anna's

screams were the wails of the strange being which had crashed into the cabin.

"Anna!" Konrad scrambled up from the ground, where he had fallen when he dodged the beast.

Hans took two steps toward the cabin, fearful, yet unable to ignore those agonized shrieks. "Anna! It will hurt Anna!"

"Not if we use our heads," said a brisk, snappish voice. Mr. Smathers trotted out of the trees at the bottom of the gully, looking fearfully grimy. His eyes were watering even more than usual.

"Don't move," he ordered. "Everyone stay right where they are and leave this to me." With that, he scooted past The Three Investigators and the astonished Hans and Konrad, and disappeared into the cabin.

16

Mr. Smathers to the Rescue

Mr. Smathers had barely entered the cabin when the terrible wailing ceased.

"There, there," the boys heard Smathers say. "I know it's bad, but you'll be all right."

Something growled.

"I know, I know," said Smathers. "But stay with me and you'll be safe."

The growling changed to a sound that was softer— almost a whimper.

"Come along, now," coaxed Mr. Smathers. "Look how you've frightened the lady. Aren't you ashamed?"

The Three Investigators looked at each other and wondered if they were dreaming.

Smathers appeared in the door of the cabin. Close behind him was the huge creature—a hulking, horrifying shape that looked half-human, half-animal. It

trailed after Smathers as meekly as a well-trained dog
might follow his master.

"We are going to the high country above the timberline," Smathers informed the astounded spectators.
"We'll be safe there. Someone had better see to the
woman. She is not in good shape."

Smathers and his strange charge went off then,
climbing rapidly through the trees. Soon they were lost
in smoke.

"Anna?" Hans kicked aside bits of the splintered
door and went into the cabin.

Konrad and The Three Investigators crowded in
after him.

Anna Schmid was crouched against the far wall of
the cabin. The little place was quite dark, but the boys
could see that despite her disheveled clothing and
tangled hair, she looked almost exactly like their host-
ess at the inn.

"Hans?" she said. "Konrad? Is it really you?"

"We have come to take you out, Anna." Hans knelt
beside her. "We must be quick. Can you stand?"

She tried, trembling and clutching at Hans. He
helped her, holding her around the waist, and Konrad
took her arm. "We will go fast, huh?" said Konrad.

She nodded. Tears began to run down her cheeks,
making little, clear tracks on her smudged face. "That
animal," she whispered. "What was that animal?"

"Let's go now, Miss Schmid," urged Jupiter. "We
can talk later."

When Anna Schmid stepped out of her prison into
the smoke-filled daylight, she was as bent and feeble as

an old woman. She had not gone many yards, however, before she lifted her head and managed to smile at Hans and Konrad. She straightened herself and squeezed her cousins' hands.

"Hurry!" pleaded Bob.

"We will hurry," said Anna.

By the time they came to the edge of the meadow, Anna was walking almost as rapidly as Pete, though she still held tight to her cousins.

They emerged from under the trees to see an awkward, big-bellied cargo plane pass overhead. It flew north, to the place where the smoke was thickest, then spewed out a cascade of liquid.

"A borate bomber," said Bob. "Hope it can hold that fire down, or we may have to hike for the timberline, too."

Pete jogged ahead of the group and was the first across the meadow. He stood at the top of the ski slope and looked down. "Hot dog!" he shouted.

"What is it?" called Jupe.

"There's a bulldozer down there cutting a firebreak. I think they've got it made. Sky Village isn't going to burn after all."

"My inn?" said Anna. "Is my inn still there?"

"A little sooty, I guess," said Pete, "but it's still there."

When Anna came to the ski slope, she hesitated for a moment to note the scene below. The bulldozer lumbered and roared as it cut a broad belt of clear earth between her inn and the fire. There was a milling, hurrying crowd of people on the road below. A second borate bomber flew overhead, then dumped its load on the flames.

Then, in an instant, there was a gust of cool air and a freshness on the meadow. The wind had changed.

"Sky Village will not burn," said Anna, and she started down the slope.

Several times she almost fell, and Hans and Konrad had to support her, but she would not hear of being left on the slope until they could get help from the village. She was shaking and stumbling when they reached the bottom, but her head was high.

Several firefighters in hard hats surged past her, intent on their jobs. Gabby Richardson was there, too, spraying the roof with a hose so that no stray ember could set fire to her inn.

Anna smiled at Richardson. "I think you are a good friend," she said.

Richardson briefly looked away from the stream of water that splashed onto the shingles above. "When I've got time," he told her, "I'd like to hear exactly what's been going on around here. Can't get a word out of that guy inside." Richardson nodded toward the inn.

"Guy inside?" said Jupiter Jones.

"Jensen," said Richardson. "He's waiting in there for you."

Hans, Konrad, Anna, and The Three Investigators went up the front steps and into the Slalom Inn.

Mr. Jensen, the bogus nature photographer, was indeed waiting. He sat on the arm of one of the big leather chairs in the living room. Opposite him, on the sofa, the woman who had called herself Anna sat and glared. Her bleached hair stood up in spikes on her head, and her eyes were red, as if she had been crying. The man named Joe Havemeyer was stretched out at her feet. He seemed to be sleeping.

"What happened?" asked Bob.

Jensen stared at Anna. "Miss Anna Schmid?" he said. He looked over at the false Anna. "Unbelievable! If it weren't for the hair, no one could tell which was which."

Bob pointed at Havemeyer. "What happened?" he said again.

Jensen grinned, and his homely face was suddenly cheerful. "Oh, I shot him," he said, "with his own tranquilizer gun!"

17

A Mirror Image

It was dark before the firefighters had the blaze contained. Even then, the inhabitants of Sky Village did not relax. Many of them stayed on the fire lines to keep an eye on the hot spots where flames still danced in the charred trees. Some stray gust of wind might still carry burning embers into the town.

At the Slalom Inn, Hans and Konrad hovered over their cousin. Anna lay on the sofa covered with an afghan, and prepared to tell her story to a young deputy sheriff who had spent a hot, tiring afternoon manning a roadblock at the foot of the mountain, turning back sightseers who wanted to get closer to the fire.

The deputy sat on a straight chair close to Anna, and scowled at Jensen. The bogus nature photographer had an air of almost hysterical joy as he kept the tranquilizer gun trained on Joe Havemeyer. Havemeyer had recovered enough to sit and glower at Jensen. The platinum-haired woman who had pretended to be Anna Schmid leaned an elbow on the dining table and kept her eyes closed. Even by lamplight she looked strangely haggard, as if she were very, very tired.

The deputy opened his notebook. "Before we begin," he said to Jensen, "put that gun away."

"I will if you put handcuffs on this crook," said Jensen. "He tried to get away earlier. He's not going to try again."

"Nobody's going to get away." The deputy touched the pistol which hung from his belt. "Put that thing down before somebody gets hurt," he ordered.

Jensen shrugged and put the tranquilizer gun in the closet. Then he took a chair from the dining table, set it before the front door, and sat down.

"That is a good idea," said Hans. He planted himself in another chair, in the doorway to the kitchen.

"Now that we've got all the exits blocked, let's get on with it," said the deputy. "Miss Schmid, your cousins tell me you wish to bring charges against Havemeyer. Would you like to tell me exactly what he's done?"

"Kidnapper!" said Konrad angrily.

"Robber!" added Hans.

"Please let Miss Schmid talk," said the deputy. "Would you begin at the beginning?"

Anna looked once at Havemeyer, then began to toy with the fringe on the afghan. "At the beginning, that man seemed very nice. He came to my inn and he wanted the best room and he looked at my ski tow. He said he is the president of a new company which makes snowmobiles, and he wants me to invest money in his company. I do not want to give him money for his company, and after a while he does not talk about it any more, but he stays on for two, three weeks.

"Then one day he sees me counting money to pay my bills. He says I should write checks and not use real money because it is safer to write checks. I told him that real money is most safe, especially my money because I keep it in my safe deposit box, and only Anna Schmid can open that box. He looked at me in a way— I don't know how to say it exactly. It was strange, and all of a sudden I was nervous."

"Is that when you hid the key?" asked Jupiter Jones.

Anna frowned. "Yes. I did not really expect trouble, but something about this man made me afraid."

"Where is the key, by the way?" asked Jupiter.

"Oh, that is very funny," said Hans. "Anna has told us what she did. She taped the key to her bedspring. Those two bad ones have been sleeping on it!"

Havemeyer made a choking sound and started to get up, but the deputy waved him back to his chair. "Go on, please, Miss Schmid," he said.

"Two or three days after we talk about the money," said Anna, "that man comes into my kitchen while I am cooking. He says he will shoot me if I do not give him the key to my safe deposit box! I think to myself, if I tell him where the key is, he will shoot me anyway, so I do not tell him."

The deputy shifted in his chair. "And then?" he said.

"I am surprised because he is not angry. He only

laughs, and he points the gun at me and he says he has time. Then he makes me go with him to the high meadow where there is that cabin the young man made. He has put a lock on the door of the cabin and he shuts me in there. For two days I do not see him at all, and I have nothing to eat but some bread and a canteen of water. Then he comes back every day and brings me food, and always he wants to know where the key is. But I do not tell him. I see that he wants very much to know, and if he finds out he will shoot me."

"I see. How long were you there, Miss Schmid?"

"Six days. Maybe seven days. It is hard to say. Then today I smelled the fire and I was much afraid. I screamed and screamed and my cousins came. My cousins and the boys—and that terrible animal. That strange little man talked to the animal and then my cousins . . . my cousins . . ." Anna Schmid put her hands over her face and began to cry.

"I will get you some water, Anna," said Hans.

"No." She wiped her cheeks with the backs of her hands. "It is all right. But how did you know where to come?"

"Jupe knew," said Hans. "Konrad and I, we thought that woman there is Anna. She looks just like the pictures you send to us."

"So she does," said Jupiter Jones, "when she wears a wig. A mirror image. I certainly believed she was Anna. It was the wedding ring and the signatures that made me realize the truth, and I'm sorry that it took me so long."

"Wedding ring?" said the deputy. "Signatures?"

"That woman practiced signing Anna Schmid's name over and over again. If she had been Anna Schmid, she wouldn't have done that. Also, her wedding ring is too big for her. She claimed she and Havemeyer were married in Lake Tahoe last week. A new bride would have a new ring which would fit. She reminded me of my Aunt Mathilda. When my aunt's been on a diet and lost a little weight, her ring is too big; she takes it off when she washes dishes and puts it on the kitchen window sill. You did that, Mrs. Havemeyer. You are really Mrs. Havemeyer, aren't you?"

"She isn't saying anything until she sees a lawyer," snarled Havemeyer, "and I'm not, either."

"I think we can reconstruct what happened," said Jupe cheerfully. "Havemeyer came here and registered at the inn. He saw that, by an uncanny coincidence, Anna Schmid was almost an exact double of his wife. This would have been a meaningless discovery were it not for the fact that Havemeyer is a criminal."

"A stock swindler," put in Jensen. "He soft-talked my sister into investing ten thousand dollars in a mining company that's been an empty hole in the ground for twenty years. Trouble is, there *is* a mine even if it's worthless, and we couldn't nail anything on him."

"And you are not a nature photographer," accused Pete.

Jensen grinned. "I own a hardware store in Tahoe. My sister spotted Havemeyer and this woman going into a coffee shop. She had a camera with her and she snapped them when they came out, and took down the license number of the car they were using. We figured the woman was another sucker he had lined up. When we checked out the license number, we got the name and address of Anna Schmid, and I came up here. I needed Havemeyer's photo because I'd never met him, and that gave me the nature photographer idea. There isn't too much reason to come to Sky Village in the summertime, so I brought my sister's camera and said I was taking pictures of the wildlife."

"You planned to warn Anna if Havemeyer tried to swindle her?" asked Bob.

"I wanted to protect her, and I also wanted to catch him in the act and get him tossed into jail. Only when I got here, he seemed to be married to Anna Schmid, and that was a new wrinkle. I went through her papers one night, and I couldn't see any evidence that he was transferring her property to his name. I couldn't figure out what the dickens he was up to."

Jupe nodded sympathetically. "So we can go back to the beginning again and imagine Havemeyer meeting Anna Schmid for the first time and seeing the incredible resemblance between Anna and his wife. At first he couldn't quite decide how to turn this to his advantage. Almost from force of habit he tried to conduct a swindle in the way he usually does. He tried to sell Anna Schmid fake stock. When she refused to buy, he wasn't disturbed. He had an ace in the hole—a wife who is so much like the real Anna Schmid that she could fool anyone. With her help, Havemeyer could get possession of everything Anna Schmid owned.

"Havemeyer stayed on at the inn until he was thoroughly acquainted with the way Anna ran things. I think we're safe in assuming that he went through the papers and ledgers in her office until he knew exactly what Anna was worth. And Anna made no secret of the fact that she kept her money in a safe deposit box. Not as convenient as a checking account, but the fake Anna could take the cash out of the box as easily as the real Anna.

"When Havemeyer was ready," Jupe continued, "he locked Anna up in the hermit's cabin and drove her car to Lake Tahoe, where he picked up fake-Anna. The two returned to Sky Village and announced that Anna Schmid had married Joe Havemeyer. Everything went smoothly, except that they couldn't find the safe deposit key.

"I am sure they were very upset when Anna's cousins arrived unannounced. However, they knew about Hans and Konrad. In their search for the key they must have gone through all of Anna's letters and seen the snapshots of her cousins.

"Havemeyer was afraid it would look odd if he wasn't cordial to his new wife's relatives, so he invited them to stay at the inn. That really put fake-Anna on the spot. But she did very well, I must say. She knew she couldn't talk German with Hans and Konrad because her accent would not be the same as the real Anna's. She *is* German, but doubtless we'll find that she comes from a part of Germany where the dialect is not the same as in Bavaria. She insisted that they all speak English so as not to exclude her husband from the conversation."

"But she still got plenty nervous," Pete put in. "She said Hans and Konrad made her nervous."

Jupiter went on, "She was also greatly upset at the thought of going to the bank and requesting a new key and having to sign for it—probably in the presence of a bank officer. The routine procedure for entering the safe deposit vault wouldn't be too difficult. She would still have to sign in, but the attendant at the vault wouldn't look closely at her signature or question her. Why should he? He knew Anna Schmid well. Getting a new key would be more complicated. She might do or say something wrong. The bank official might carefully compare her signature to the signature on Anna Schmid's registration.

"So fake-Anna became nervous about signing Anna Schmid's name. She apologized too much to the man who delivered the cement, and she and Joe Havemeyer quarreled. Havemeyer made her practice writing Anna's name and he got us out of the house when she did it. But we saw her "homework" paper. Then I knew that she was not really Anna, and I knew why Havemeyer went to the meadow every day."

The deputy closed his notebook and stared at Anna Schmid. He then turned and looked at fake-Anna. "If I weren't seeing it with my own eyes, I wouldn't believe that two human beings could be so much alike," he said. "But what about that gun—the tranquilizer gun? Was that the gun Havemeyer used to threaten you, Miss Schmid?"

"No," said Anna. "The gun he used was a shotgun."

"It's in the closet," Pete told the deputy.

The door behind Jensen's chair rattled. Jensen stood up, put the chair to one side, and opened the door.

Mr. Smathers trotted into the room. He was smoke-stained and incredibly grimy, but very brisk and bright. "Everything's fine here, I see," he said. Then his eyes lighted on Anna Schmid lying on the sofa, and on fake-Anna crouched near the table. He saw the deputy with his notebook, and Hans grimly blocking the kitchen doorway. "My word!" he said.

"It's pretty complicated, Mr. Smathers," Bob told him. "We'll explain it to you later."

"Does he have anything to do with this?" asked the deputy, nodding toward Smathers.

"I hardly think so," said Jupiter. "I believe Mr. Smathers is exactly what he claims to be—a man who can talk to animals."

"And they listen," declared Smathers cheerfully.

"Sure, sure," said the deputy. "Now maybe somebody will tell me why this guy had a tranquilizer gun?"

"Hideous, isn't it?" said Mr. Smathers. "Almost worse than a conventional firearm. Imagine wanting to capture a wild creature and put it in a cage. Disgraceful!"

The deputy's expression was one of total bewilderment. "You mean that in addition to everything else, this man was out to bag a bear?"

"Not a bear," said Pete.

Mr. Smathers chuckled. "Would you believe, officer, that Mr. Havemeyer thinks there is a monster of some type on this mountain? He harbored the idiotic idea that he could capture a being unknown to science and exhibit it to the public, doubtless charging a fee for anyone who wanted to look at it!"

"A monster?" said the deputy. "The guy's got cracks in his brain!"

"Indeed he does," said Mr. Smathers. "We all know there are no such things as monsters, don't we?"

The Three Investigators gaped at the weedy little man. Mr. Smathers smiled and went upstairs.

18

Mr. Hitchcock Learns a Secret

Two days after they returned to Rocky Beach, The Three Investigators called on Alfred Hitchcock at his office.

"I see that you have made the newspapers again," said the famous motion-picture director. "I assume that you have written up this entire astounding affair. What are you going to call it? The Mystery of the Mirror Image?"

"We thought The Mystery of Monster Mountain might be a better title," said Jupiter Jones.

"Monster Mountain?" Mr. Hitchcock frowned. "I have carefully gone over every news story on the kidnapping of Anna Schmid, and I have seen no mention whatever of a Monster Mountain."

"We didn't tell the reporters everything," said Bob, and he handed a file across the desk to the director.

"I should have guessed it," said Mr. Hitchcock. He opened the file and began to read.

The boys waited in silence until Mr. Hitchcock finished reading the notes that Bob had made on the case. When Mr. Hitchcock closed the file, he nodded. "Clever deductions, Jupiter Jones," he said. "And there really was a monster?"

"We saw it," Jupe told him. "But who would believe us? Hans and Konrad and Anna saw it, too, but they don't even believe it. Hans and Konrad quickly decided that they'd seen a bear on its hind legs. Anna has buried the whole episode in the back of her mind and refuses to talk about it. And Mr. Smathers will never tell." Jupiter shrugged.

Pete explained, "After the deputy took away Havemeyer and his wife, Mr. Smathers talked to us. He told us that if we said anything to the newspapers or the sheriff about the monster, he'd deny it and say that it was a bear we saw in the hermit's cabin. It would be his word against ours—and no one believes wild stories from kids."

"So it's a secret," said Mr. Hitchcock. "I appreciate the fact that you've shared it with me. I suppose it was Smathers who punched you, Jupiter, and who erased the creature's tracks near the earthquake fracture?"

"He admitted it," said Jupe. "But, again, he said he'd deny it if we mentioned the incident to the authorities. Whatever that creature is, Mr. Smathers wants to protect it, and the only way he can protect it is to conceal the fact that it even exists."

"Quite right," said Mr. Hitchcock. "If people knew

there was a monster on the mountain, I am sure that numbers of men like Havemeyer would be out with tranquilizer guns hunting for it."

"In a way, I'm glad it all turned out as it did," said Bob. "I spent a couple of hours at the library last night, checking out some of the California folklore books. For years there have been reports of strange tracks in the Sierras and the Cascade Range. We have our own version of the Abominable Snowman, I guess, except that nobody's ever been able to prove that he really exists. He stays back in the wild country, out of sight."

"We can assume that the one we saw came down to the inn to get food, just as the bears did," said Jupe. "Mr. Smathers saw its tracks in the yard two days before we arrived at Sky Village. That very day, Havemeyer bought the tranquilizer gun, and the next day he had men up from Bishop to dig out that so-called swimming pool. Smathers guessed what he was up to, and he started hiking all through the high country, trying to find the creature and warn it. He passed the hermit's cabin several times, but since he didn't speak, Anna didn't know anyone was nearby."

"Poor Anna," said Mr. Hitchcock. "What a dreadful experience that must have been."

"She was pretty well recovered by the time we left," Pete said. "And Hans and Konrad had a terrific visit with her. They like the real Anna much better than fake-Anna. She made lots of hot chocolate and pastries for them, and they yanked the wooden forms out of that hole in her back yard and filled it in. No swimming pool. No bear pit. Mr. Smathers was tickled pink."

"I am sure he was," said Mr. Hitchcock. "Mr. Jensen must also have been highly gratified to see the man who swindled his sister put behind bars."

"You can say that again," said Pete. "He gets the cold shudders when he thinks of what might have happened to the real Anna Schmid while he was hanging around trying to protect the fake Anna Schmid. Havemeyer wasn't always a con man. He's been arrested for armed robbery, and once he shot a bank guard. The man didn't die, but probably only because Havemeyer's a bad shot. So he can be violent."

"Mr. Jensen is also glad that Havemeyer didn't uncover his game," added Bob. "Jensen could have been in great danger himself. He said he'd had quite enough violence after being hit the night he took a picture of the bear."

"Why did he shoot that photograph?" asked Mr. Hitchcock. "And who hit him?"

"As I guessed," said Jupiter, "Mr. Jensen snapped the bear merely to keep up the pretense that he was a wildlife photographer. He told us he looked out his window that night and saw a bear coming to the trash cans and decided the shot was too convenient to pass up. We figure it must have been the monster who hit him. Mr. Smathers claims the flash going off scared the beast, and it struck out instinctively. We're only guessing here. Jensen now blames the attack on a second bear."

"Is Jensen not in on the secret of Monster Mountain?"

Bob shook his head. "There wasn't any need to tell

him. And he probably wouldn't have believed us anyway. I don't think anyone besides you would believe
us!" The investigator grinned.

"And you're pleased about that, I see," said Mr.
Hitchcock.

Bob nodded. "I guess Mr. Smathers has made a con-
vert out of me. I sure didn't like the looks of that animal, but it would be kind of a shame to stick it in a
cage and have people pay fifty cents a head for the
privilege of getting a peek at it. And it's kind of fun to
think that there *is* something back there in the hills
that we haven't classified and cataloged and counted. I
mean . . . well . . ."

"You are a romantic," concluded Mr. Hitchcock.
"You are a preserver of nature's unsolved mysteries. I
quite agree with you. Few places are unexplored
today, and few things are unexplained. We need the
unknown and legendary creatures to stir our imagination."

He stood up and handed the file back to Bob. "Long
live the monster of Monster Mountain," he said, "and
if I were you, I would not hesitate to publish the file on
the case of Anna Schmid. The monster will safely re-
main a legend. As you keep pointing out, no one will
believe you!"